THE

TUNNEL

By Amara Bea Glavin

1:
CHESS

The job was stupid. All we had to do was go to some bougie restaurant, convince the people we were some charity that helped kids with cancer, and pick up a check from some billionaire. Maybe he was a millionaire, but that's usually Paul's responsibility. Details weren't always my thing. But of course, Paul's bossiness got in the way. He made a big deal out of everything, and just like always, little puppy dog Ren copied him, trying to prove himself.

My position within this job was to do the actual flirting, and by flirting, I mean twirling my long brown hair to the point where he physically wrote the check. That's right, I was about to go to dinner with this man, and I was ninety percent sure he was in his eighties, and ten percent sure he was in his nineties.

He would probably say something like, "Miss Chessy, you look so breathtaking on this lovely evening."

Then I would say something like, "Oh please, call me Chess. That's how much I hate my middle and first name, because if you call me Harriet, you will lose your testicles." Or at least that's what I said to most people. Except in this scenario, I wouldn't be giving him my real name.

My dress was itchier than it usually was, but Ren kept telling me to stop complaining because he needed to "concentrate on driving." To be fair, he was a terrible driver, but I was worse, and Paul was the only British member of the team, so he couldn't drive on the right side of the road for shit. So, I guess technically, he was the worst out of all of us.

Never in this career have I ever been excited for events that required wearing a dress. It was just the three of us that ran cons together, and I was the only woman. I was also creeping up on turning thirty, and heels hadn't been my thing since junior prom. Other than that, I did enjoy the occasional flirtation with men my age, but I highly doubted this was gonna be one of those nights. This was an "In and out" kinda job.

"Anybody fancy a drink?" Paul asked.

"Welp, that depends," I responded. "Are you gonna give me that crap you usually drink, or are you gonna give me alcohol?"

"Hey, crappy drinks are one of my favorite things about America."

"Because it represents everything about this country?"

"Hey!" Ren finally chimed in. I almost forgot he was there. That wasn't a rarity. "Don't say shit like that. He's lucky to be here."

"Nah," I waved off. "He's lucky he found us."

To be fair, he was. Ren was essentially my assistant when Paul found us through a friend, and we all decided to work as a team. Ren was the technician, I was the influencer, and Paul was the muscles, but only if we needed him to be. He was also the bossiest person I knew, but I usually ignored that. In the last year, we had made almost three million dollars. That's a little less than one million each, since about fifteen percent goes to our "agent," John. He was always amazing at finding us the perfect cons. He deserved to be in jail way more than the rest of us. But, besides being cons, we were basically normal citizens. We paid our taxes, and we followed most laws. It makes getting caught a hell of a lot less likely.

I took one of Paul's crappy drinks just to calm my nerves. Now, don't get me all wrong here. I didn't necessarily get *nervous* for jobs, but rather *annoyed* at how much effort I had to put into them. This was one of those times. If we were at a club, and I was in ripped-up jean shorts and high-heeled sneakers, we would be having a different conversation.

"How drunk can I be for this encounter?"

"Only a little, I would say," Paul snapped. "The man likes a poised woman."

"That was more of a rhetorical question. Imma drink as much as I want tonight."

"Chess, I promise you it won't take that long," said Ren, knowing how impatient I usually was when I was about to put on a show. "You won't have the time to drink that heavily."

"That's a matter of opinion."

Finally, we rolled up to the restaurant. It was a hell of a lot bigger than I imagined. We'd done quite a bit of business in other fancy dining places around Atlanta, but this was a new place. *Ontario's,* it read at the top in flashing green lights. My ignorant ass wasn't sure if that was Italian or not, so I didn't bother getting excited about fettuccine alfredo.

"Here we are. Do we need to go over the plan again?" Ren asked as if he were in charge.

"Do you even know the plan, Ren?" Paul asked. "You're just staying in the car and listening, remember, mate?"

"Yup, as usual," I added. Sometimes I was for sure too mean to Ren, but he knew I adored him. It was all about balance in our relationship. Paul, on the other hand, we mainly just had back and forth competitions on who could talk the loudest without making ourselves sound like smokers. "Okay, mic check, Ren?"

"Check," he said, popping his finger up.

"Check for me," I said.

"Paul?" Ren asked.

"Checkmate," he said as usual, thinking it was hilarious. "Don't fuck it up, love."

"Don't be rude," I, of course, said louder than he did.

For tonight, I chose the most comfortable high heels that I had just in case I had to run. Getting chased by the cops wasn't a likely event, but it had happened once or twice before.

The wind almost took out my cheap curls that I probably should have sprayed more, but I already looked stupid enough. *Ugh*, I felt so out of place. Once I stepped into what looked like a palace, I immediately wanted to drop my fake posture and whack every person in here upside the head. These kinds of people waste their money on the stupidest shit. The money that I made was put towards experiences like traveling and exciting events. But by all means, spend some money on disgusting food instead of getting a delicious burger at Burger King. Maybe that was just the broke teenager in me talking.

"Do you have a reservation, Miss?" the hostess asked me.

"No, I'm meeting someone. Last name Beau." This maybe nineteen-year-old girl looked at me as if I was about to meet the hottest date on the face of the planet, but I surprised myself by suppressing the disgusted look on my face.

The place was so big that I could have taken the highway to our table. On our way over the hostess mentioned that her name was Sammy and that Bryan would be our server for that night as if I knew who that was. Once we finished our journey and finally reached our table, Sammy presented me to Mr. Patrick Beau, one of the richest men in Atlanta, and just like most rich white men, he was as bald as a naked mole rat.

"Miss Rose," he said, standing up and kissing my hand. Wow, already in need of hand sanitizer.

"Oh please, call me Rita." I came up with this *Rita Rose* nonsense of a name that sounded both stupid and rad at the same time, and honestly, I'm proud of it.

"Well, then. What will you be drinking tonight, Rita?"

"Any glass of red would truly hit the spot for me tonight." He called over the waiter as if he was the owner, which now that I think of it, he might have been.

We discussed some nonsense such as previous business deals and stupid stories that he thought were amusing. A few times, he tried to divert the conversation to politics, but I made a sharp turn away from that shit.

The restaurant was the most un-American thing I'd ever seen in my life, and by that I, of course, mean the portion sizes were meant for a baby that always pushed their food off the table no matter how small it was. Also, the food looked like it was only various types of meatloaf. I would have given anything to record this man trying to define the word "Vegetarian."

"So, why don't we talk over some charitable details? Shall we?" Mr. Beau suggested. I was honestly surprised he was the one to bring it up first. I was planning on badgering him all the way through dessert.

"That would be lovely," I responded in the most rich-person voice I could produce. I was actually kinda getting the hang of it.

"Well, I-"

"Excuse me, Sir and Madame," I heard a familiar voice say, literally right next to me. I didn't need to look over to see who it was, but I couldn't blow my cover either. To my left, stood the six-foot-four asshole known as Paul. This was not part of the plan, but per usual, he wanted to steal the show that nobody had tickets to. "Would you like to try tonight's samples?"

"No, thank you," I said, still trying not to blow my cover. Paul was wearing the most ridiculous uniform that was three sizes too small. The brown apron looked like it was gonna pop off him.

"The samplers already?" Mr. Beau inquired. "Those weren't supposed to come out for another twenty minutes." He checked his oddly-colored pocket watch that read *Patience* on it in beautiful calligraphy, just to make sure he wasn't going crazy even though he probably would've needed a lot more clarification than that.

"My apologies, Sir. I shall be back soon." And just like that, the idiot left. Paul didn't usually like to over exaggerate his Britishness, but let me tell you, that was extreme and pretty cringeworthy.

"Anyways," Mr. Beau steered back to our original conversation. "Tell me a little bit more about the charity."

"Well, I do hope you had some time to look at the website. It still surprises me that that was one of our biggest investments while planning this con. Anyways, we help children and teenagers get off the streets and out of abusive homes. Right now, our biggest project is building or buying a shelter for more children to live in. Right now, many are in foster homes, but I'm sure you know that those homes can be just as bad as their original ones."

He definitely didn't know that, but I shouldn't have been talking since I didn't know those statistics either until I looked it up before arriving.

"Of course. So horrible. What would you need to cover the costs?" Mr. Beau asked.

"Oh, I don't expect you to cover the entire cost of the building." Of course, I did, but I couldn't possibly be so obvious.

"I insist. It's no problem whatsoever." He started to take out his checkbook and pen which probably cost more than my loft.

"That's very generous of you. It would be about eight million dollars." If he had food or a drink in his mouth, he would have choked. Maybe I shouldn't have said it so matter-of-factly.

"Are you absolutely positive about that?"

"Mr. Beau," I took his hand as if I was telling him his wife just died of cancer. "There are so many children that need your help. Plus, you can put this as the biggest tax donation write-off of your career."

If he wasn't already so old, I would have been able to tell for certain if he was blushing or not, but I'm pretty sure he was. As kind as he seemed, he was probably a secret narcissist. Classic old white man wanting to get attention for helping children when they don't actually care. They truly were the easiest targets.

"You're a very good influencer, Miss Rose. Did you know that?" The old man cracked a smile as if he was giving me the best compliment in the entire world. If only he knew.

I put my dainty hand to my heart as if I'd never heard that before in my life and said, "Why thank you. That is the sweetest thing to say, and don't worry. Your name will be all over this building. Everyday children will be reminded of what you did for them. They will never forget a single detail about you."

His chest almost sprouted to the ceiling like Tarzan making his monkey noises. It was like this was his first donation he had ever made as a rich person.

He finished writing the check before we made a toast to the children that didn't exist and had a few more drinks.

"Chess," I heard in my earpiece. Ren's voice over a radio was truly an obnoxious sound. "Chess, are you there? You have the check, right? Time to go."

"Shall we order dessert?" Mr. Beau asked.

"Oh, no I couldn't possibly impose." Although the brownie sundae looked more mouthwatering than a shirtless Michael B. Jordan at that moment. Then again, I kinda wanted to make the boys take me to Uno's.

"Are you sure? Everything is my treat, you know?" Ugh, this man really needed to stop being so nice after I just stole eight million dollars from him.

I stood up, drunkenly rewrapped my handbag around my wrist and said, "I'm absolutely positive. Trust me, you have done enough. And besides, I'm due to wake up early tomorrow morning and celebrate with all of the ladies on our newest victory."

"Just ladies?"

For some reason that was always a verbal reflex for me. "The ladies". Before Ren and Paul, I had usually only worked with women while I was a nurse. I was used to it. So, at this moment, I just completely made up that it was a female led group.

"Oh, yes. We are completely made up of women. All paid." Okay, maybe that was a dumb lie, but I was a better improvisor when I had more details.

"Funny, I could have sworn I saw men up on your website."

"Ohhhh. You see. So irresponsible of us. We haven't updated that website in quite some time. Anyway, I have a big responsibility of bringing this to the bank before I lose it. Have a beautiful night, Mr. Beau, and thank you again. We will be in touch soon."

If this were a movie, I probably would have done one of those black and white acting techniques where I wipe my forehead from how close that was. But hot damn, that was a close one. Maybe I was getting too confident in myself.

"Please tell me you're on your way out of there," Ren shouted into my ear.

"I've got it," I said. "I'm walking out. And by the way. Paul, you're an idiot. You know that, right?"

"What?!" Paul exclaimed. "You were nervous! It was our biggest scam yet! I thought you would chuckle."

"Yes, hilarious."

Before I exited the front door, I looked back to see if Mr. Beau was still looking at me. He was...obviously. Most people would keep staring from the way my ass looked in this dress, no matter how awkward I felt. I gave him one last little wave like the Queen of England with a little kiss and walked out the door. What can I say? Job well done.

"Welp, that was rough," said Chess, as she nearly got naked, ripping her dress off. "I vote next time Ren does the sexy talk in the sexy dress."

"You know I would," Ren replied, most likely being serious.

"So, exactly how drunk are you right now?" I asked Chess.

"Not as drunk as I would like to be. Where's that crap you like to drink?" I gave her more of the beer I always have, which I'll admit was quite rubbish, but it was all I could afford as a teenager in East London. "Please tell me we're going home."

"Stop your whimpering. The night is still young, love. There's still so much to do." I truly enjoyed annoying Chess with my cheekiness in the nighttime. She was the definition of a morning person, which really didn't go well with her drinking problem.

"That might be true, but what I want to do is deposit this check, divide our cuts, and watch some Netflix. Is that too much to ask?"

"Actually," Ren squeaked his way back into the conversation. "When he says there's still so much to do, what he means is we got a call. We have another job."

"What?" Chess was even more ghastly looking than when she found out she had to bring out her evening gown. "From who?"

"Well, like usual, the call was from John, but he didn't say who it was for."

John was basically our middle man, or our agent if we were film stars. He took a small cut from cons he would get for us and usually handled our taxes. We had a rather formal business going.

"He knows I don't like it when he does that," I told the rest. That old chap didn't usually pull this rubbish, but it's not as if you could really trust anyone in this business anyway. "What's the job? Did he tell you that at least?"

"Almost," Ren answered. "It was something about tricking some old guy into thinking his antique was worth less than it was, then we can buy it off him and resell it for more."

That was a new one.

"How is that going to work?" Chess asked.

"Dementia." Chess and I sighed, suddenly understanding. Damn, taking advantage of a guy with dementia was also a new one. Especially since Chess used to be a nurse. She probably wasn't going to be thrilled about this one. John seemed to be progressively getting harsher and harsher by the job. It was usually one of us that had dementia, and a GoFundMe page would be set up in our honor. That usually only got us about three grand each.

"Why do we have to go tonight?"

Ren did an annoyed and pitiful groan before he answered, "That's just what we were told. I don't know. We were told to rarely ask questions, remember? But never mind that. It'll be fun."

"Funny." Oh boy here it comes. "I do remember that. It was almost like I was the one who taught you that when you were MY assistant."

Chess always had a habit of reminding us that she was the original member of this company, or so we called it. She wasn't in charge anymore. We considered that to be John, but she usually had a sense of superiority towards us. Even though she was probably a decade younger than both Ren and I, or so we thought. She never liked to talk about her birthday or her age.

"Look," Ren started, disregarding Chess's remark. "We have a call with John in forty-five minutes. Let's get some food in the meantime, and Chess, you can sober up a bit."

"Welp. No promises of that happening," said Chess as she continued to chug a beer.

After we deposited the check, we stopped at Burger King since Chess requested it five times, and ate enough for at least ten people. I'd always been in charge of finances, so after I got the notification that the money went through, I sent John and the rest their cuts. Apparently, this made John more eager to fill us in on our next job. He rang us up, just like he said not even five minutes later.

"Please tell us this is going to be a quick job," I complained to him when I picked up my mobile.

"Define quick," he responded like the dick that he always was.

"Faster than Ren in bed, so pretty quick!" Chess yelled through the phone, somehow hearing our conversation.

"Christ. Put me on speaker before Chess gives herself nodes." I did so while staring Chess down for being the attention seeker that she was. "First things first." That's how he started every phone call with us and probably with everyone else in his life. "There's this old man about an hour and a half outside of Atlanta -"

"AN HOUR AND A HALF?" Chess interrupted as usual. She had this thing about interrupting men just to get even for their audacity of doing so to women.

"Chess, you'll survive. A'ight, next. This guy wants to secretly get a quote on how much one of his antique chairs will go for. My guess is it's worth maybe a million, but we're going to say it's worth less than what it is."

Genius.

"So," said Ren. "We buy this chair, sell it for a lot more at what it's actually worth, and get a profit."

"Bingo."

We stumbled through a few more details while Ren kept trying to impress John with how much of the conversation he was comprehending. Chess wasn't acting like such an angel either, of course. As usual, she repeatedly acted like she was too good for the conversation and already knew everything. But it all came down to this; Essentially, Chess would be the antique expert, I would be her assistant, and as usual, Ren would stay in the car and be on the phone as the dealer.

"So why is it secret?" Chess asked.

"His wife apparently doesn't want to sell it, but money is tight for them or something, so he's going behind her back."

"Ahh, I see."

Something was fishy. On the other hand, there was always some nutter who wanted us to do some odd job, but still something was off. I think Chess noticed it as well.

"What's this guy's name?" Ren asked.

12

"Samuel something," John replied. Odd. John usually knew all the details, and if he didn't, he would often make something up like Julia Child or something like that since he thought he was the most hilarious wanker to walk the planet.

"Everything alright, John?" Ren asked. His suspicions were growing with us, he was just a little slow.

"And what kind of chair is it?" I asked. Luckily for the group, I grew up in an antique shop that my parents owned. Now, I was no expert, but it was probably why John took this job in the first place. He was a cautious guy. Very smart and with outrageous resources and connections. Not as tech savvy as Ren, but more logical, and skillful in the art of deceiving.

"Sounds good to us," said Ren. "We'll call you when it gets done. I'm putting in the address right now." And he hung up.

"Something's weird, guys," said Ren. I didn't like him using the word "weird". Truthfully, I didn't like any American using that word. They were some of the strangest and most outrageous human beings to steal a country. The way they behaved and endlessly bickered baffled me, but that was just my opinion. Ren however was a special kind of weird. With his lack of social skills and eye contact, he had no right calling someone or something weird, but again, just my completely accurate ideas and assumptions.

"Imma look this place up," said Chess, pulling out her phone.

"Look," I said, trying to get their attention. "I'm sure everything is fine. Maybe we just need to be more discreet about this job. Maybe there are just some dodgy people that we need to avoid. If something goes wrong, we'll just leg it and get out of there."

Ren immediately agreed with an aggressive "Of course!" while Chess brutally rolled her eyes and nodded her head. That was her usual response as you could probably guess.

One time, John assigned us a job where we ripped off this junkie who was absolutely bonkers. We didn't know her name. We only got a picture of what she looked like, and we gave her baby powder instead of cocaine and got a thousand dollars in return. I knew we could handle a ninety-something-year old chap, but we would just have to see.

3:
REN

The whole drive to this place, Chess and Paul wouldn't shut up about how quick they wanted to do this job. I kept saying to them, "I think it'll be fine, and if not y'all will survive." Apparently, that wasn't reassuring enough for them.

One time when we were on a job a few years ago, Chess had to wait outside a hospital asking for donations for children's care. After an hour of being there, she came up with some sob story for a doctor about her child dying of cancer or something like that, even though we hadn't planned it. Luckily, the doctor didn't look this fake daughter up, and we got away with over a thousand dollars just because Chess wanted to get out of there as quickly as possible. That woman couldn't stay still for shit.

With me driving, I managed to shave off almost a half an hour of our trip. The time was almost 12:30 a.m. when we finally reached the house, but upon first sight, it looked less like a house and more like a mixture between an abandoned mental hospital and a miniature version of Hogwarts. I wasn't sure which part of the mixture made me more nervous.

"This is it?" Chess asked with pure disdain.

"Bugger, I hope not," Paul laughed.

"Come on," I said. "We'll be fine. Let's go."

I texted John to let him know that we had arrived and we would let him know the second the job was done. For reasons unknown to probably all of us, the entire neighborhood creeped us out to the point that we were afraid to shut the car doors. It was dark, after all, and this part of town was beyond unfamiliar to us. From the looks of it, it was probably even more unknown to any G.P.S. on this planet.

"It doesn't look like anyone's home," said Paul. "Anyone see a -" My guess was that he was about to ask if anyone saw a light, but before he could finish, it looked like almost every light in the house popped on all at once.

"So, is everyone ready?" I asked the others.

"No shit," Chess so politely replied.

I reached to knock on the door until Paul beat me to it. He used his dark muscular arms and pounded on the door three times. No answer. Three more times. Still no answer. I joined in with him while Chess stood behind us, annoyed by our metaphorical dick-measuring competition that we were used to having. That is, until we realized that the door was just stuck and it opened easily after we pushed through.

"I'll go in first," I said. I wanted to do at least one thing first, and I really wasn't up for Paul trying to scare me and then call me a wuss.

To our surprise, the interior part of the house seemed significantly less creepy than its exterior. Everything simply looked old, or antique. For a while, we walked around the living room in silence. Checking everything out, taking in the view.

For us, there was something about admiring other people's wealth. We all had wealth of our own, of course, being in this line of work. But when you thought about it, this was exactly why we did what we did. We were *obsessed* with admiration. Mainly, we loved to admire ourselves, because of how often we compared ourselves to other people. It resembled something along the lines of, "This person has a golden shower curtain; therefore, I must have a completely golden bathroom." We couldn't get over it. Saying that we were better than the people we admired and surrounded ourselves with is what fed our souls.

"Anybody hear anything?" Paul asked, breaking the silence.

"Nada." Chess responded.

We figured we would hear footsteps or something in the house, or even next door, but there wasn't any noise coming from surrounding properties either. What was this place?

"Maybe he's not home and the lights just turned on automatically," I suggested, knowing immediately Chess was going to make fun of me.

"In the whole house?" She questioned. "Yeah, because that makes sense." See?

Paul mainly kept to himself, for once. He stood in the corner playing with some sort of glass ball that was probably not supposed to be thrown back and forth, yet he was doing it anyways, because why not?

"Geez," I cringed, fighting the urge to go over to him and rip it out of his hand. "Be careful with that."

"Mate, I'm not gonna break anything." He didn't even make eye contact with me, but to my surprise, his tone wasn't as attitudinal as it usually was. Gee, thanks, Paul.

Then suddenly, I heard a creak coming from the stairs behind me, but when I turned around, there was no old man walking down the stairs.

"Chess, no!" That idiot tried to creep up the stairs, but any fool should have figured that was going too far. "We're gonna get a shotgun pulled on us!"

"Stop being so paranoid. He must know we're here." One thing that Chess *loved* to do was to defend her actions verbally, but not follow through with them. In this case, she thought she was completely in her right to go up this mysterious man's stairs, but she walked right back down and didn't go through with it. She just didn't want to actually admit that she was wrong and stupid.

"Should we yell up?" Paul asked, still tossing around some decoration in his hand.

"I think this is a set up." Chess always thought it was a set up, but part of me appreciated her caution. We still had never been caught on a job, but other times it made jobs go by painfully slow. How many times could one do a full background and security check of a building and check on everyone who has ever worked in it?

Suddenly, before Chess could storm out, cursing at us to leave with her, there was the sound of a floorboard creaking in what was probably the kitchen.

"Did you hear that?" I asked.

"Unfortunately," Paul loudly whispered.

"It's probably just a cat." Chess almost laughed. "Then again, that's what people usually say right before they get eaten in horror movies." And then she laughed for real.

"Sir?" Paul yelled out, probably forgetting his name.

"Samuel?" This was an appropriate time for me to rub it in his face that I paid more attention than he did, but he didn't even look at me or notice my "Really?" face.

No more sounds came from the kitchen, or anywhere for that matter. At first, we carefully and slowly crept toward the dark area. There was only a small, turquoise archway that led to it, but past the archway was pure, midnight black, or at least that was all that I could see. Nonetheless, after I became overly annoyed by Paul's obnoxiously loud breathing that I was just now noticing, I shook off most of my fear and quickly tiptoed to the archway, ready to search for a light switch.

"Dude! Be careful," said Chess.

Thanks. So useful, I thought.

I felt around behind the wall and in front of it. Nothing. That seemed odd, but maybe the only light was on a ceiling fan or something of the sort that was only operable from the actual fan itself. Boy, I really didn't want to fully immerse myself in the pitch black, but I didn't want to know what the repercussions would be if I didn't. Chess would never let me live it down.

First, I stuck my hand out just to make sure there wasn't an old man standing right in front of me. Who knew where that idea came from, but considering the eccentric behavior going on in this place, I found it to be a reasonable precaution. I let my hand whack from side to side a few times, and when I finally accepted that nothing was going to jump out in front of me, I took a step forward. Heel first, then toes, but the second my dress shoe flattened into the floor, something shifted.

I couldn't tell exactly what it was, but I could have sworn it was almost as if the floor...broke. Maybe something just slipped from under me. My next guess would have been a crack in the tile, but before I could even suggest that to my brain, something else got in the way.

"Oh my God, guys?" I could hear Chess yelling. She probably clung onto something as the earth began to shake.

"Earthquake! Duck!" Paul shouted.

Duck? Duck where? I thought. *How would that help us?*

"Don't duck, run!" I yelled, but by the time I reached the door, it wouldn't budge. "Come on, come on!" I didn't give up like I often would. Now was not the time. The catastrophe quickly escalated. The earth was about to slip from under me at any moment. We were stuck.

"Ren, DUCK!" Paul yelled again. I had no choice. What else was I supposed to do? Paul was right for once.

Like one is supposed to do on an airplane, I put both of my hands on the back of my head as my chin dug into my chest. But there was something weird and off about this earthquake. To be honest, I hadn't felt many earthquakes in my life, but this one felt more like a giant vibrator was stuck underneath the house. The vibration was quick, and boy, it gave me a headache faster than Paul could give me one.

The shaking had only lasted a few seconds, but it had already dragged on for too long. No earthquakes around here lasted that long. What was going on?

I knew I had to check on my coworkers and see if they were still okay, even though the shaking was making it hard to see. However, when I looked up to see the living room, I almost had to do a double take to see what was happening. My eyes were obviously not in complete focus, but they weren't deceiving me. The walls were crumbling to bits.

It was as if piles of dust were falling from the walls, or like the house was a sand castle with paint on it and it was all just chipping away. The color of the dust was the most alarming and grim part. It was black. No other colors, just black. Most hair colors, fabrics, and sand all have layers of color. Not this stuff, and it was growing heavier and breaking away from the walls at an increasing speed.

"We gotta get out of here!" I yelled, trying to see my colleagues through the dark vibration. I ran to the back door while still covering my head with one arm. Locked. Maybe jammed, but probably locked. I turned around to see Chess and Paul at the other end of the room trying to open the front door. Locked. We were trapped.

"WHAT IS THIS?!" Paul hollered.

"GET UNDER SOMETHING!" Chess screamed back instead of answering, though nobody had expected her to.

There wasn't much to get under, or at least I didn't see many tables or shelves to protect us, but I ran to the middle of the room, right next to the couch, trying to get as far away from walls as I could.

After a long few minutes, the racket almost became a white noise. Maybe *grey* would be a better word for it, but it wouldn't stop, and it was perfectly consistent. No stopping and starting. It just. Kept. Going.

Nothing had hurt me or even brushed up against me yet. I figured I should probably check to see if Paul and Chess were okay, but when I looked up, they weren't in my view. I couldn't see them, but Chess and Paul weren't my main concern when I noticed my new surroundings. That's correct. *New* surroundings. I was no longer in the house anymore, and when I heard Chess and Paul groaning and swearing, I was happy to say *we* were no longer in the house or wherever it was we were.

"Is everyone okay?" I asked since no one else did.

"We're fine." I heard Chess say, even though she was barely visible.

Maybe we were transported, or maybe the walls revealed what was under them. Did we fall? Did the room transform? Either way, there was nothing but dark, dirty rocks all around us. We were in a cave. A long, yet small cave that had a tiny spec of light at the end of the tunnel. That was the only reason we were somewhat able to see. Just from that penny-sized beam of light.

"What...happened?" Paul asked. Funny. He was always the macho man with all the answers.

"Who cares? Let's just get out of here!" Chess exclaimed, not even looking at us and running toward the light. I almost forgot. She was claustrophobic. This ought to be good.

"Wait, Chess! Stop it!" I snapped. "This could be some sort of trap. We have to be careful. Does anyone have service? We need to call John, now!"

While Chess kept pacing back and forth and senselessly scratching her entire body, we all checked our phones. They wouldn't even turn on, let alone allow us to make a phone call.

"What the bloody hell is this place?" Paul kept his stance wide and his eyes open. He was right to. Anything could jump out of a dead-end tunnel with nothing but rock-solid stones surrounding us and only one way out. Anything.

Chess stopped her scratching and pacing before she moved onto trying to break through the cave walls. Nothing was moving. There was barely even sand to kick around on the floor.

"Guys, there's only one way out." I told them. "We can figure out what happened when we get out, or on the way. Whatever. We just gotta keep moving. Standing here won't do us any good."

"Welp, no arguments there," Chess sassed. And so, she led us on our way through the dark, cold tunnel.

4:
CHESS

The tiny spec of light at the end of the tunnel stayed exactly the same size and didn't disappear or blink for even a millisecond after we walked for probably hours. I was too hungry and tired to even look at my watch to keep track of the time. My knees ached, but my head hurt the most out of anything. Ren kept telling me to breathe, but I kept reminding him that I would be dead and wouldn't have to listen to his shit if I wasn't breathing already.

"Anybody need a break?" Paul asked.

"No," I replied, rubbing my head. "What I need is to get out of here."

Ren vigorously snapped his head in various directions around the cave and said, "There must be an opening somewhere. Maybe we just can't see it."

"It can't possibly be that easy," I said, always thinking everything was against me.

Ren kept making himself look like an idiot for the next few hours as we chugged and pushed ourselves along. Eventually, somebody had to admit what we were trying to avoid. As usual, I got too impatient to wait anymore.

"I gotta pee like a mother fucker," I finally admitted.

"I think we all do, love," said Paul, out of breath. "Come on. Let's just all be weird and face away from each other. Clearly, Paul missed a few things about the female anatomy in sex education class, but I tried my best to be as discrete as possible.

After we finished our business, I was desperate for hand sanitizer. God, I hate germs. Then, I felt more gross than before. It was gonna be a long trip.

"Ahhhhh!" Ren screamed. It was too dark to notice what had happened, but I thought I saw him hopping on one leg.

"What?" Paul tried to yell over Ren's screaming. "What did you do? What's wrong?"

"I think I stepped into a ditch and twisted my ankle." Shit. Normally he wouldn't be screaming like a baby *that* much, but since he was, that probably meant it was his bad ankle that he twisted. The left one. Last year, he broke it in his car accident after running away from a very angry client. Try telling that story to an insurance agent.

"Come on, come on. Sit down," I told him, trying to calm him. "Let me see - or feel it." All my years as a nurse made this line a reflex for me.

Nothing felt broken, but I could feel the torn ligament. It popped out like Shaq's penis. He wasn't walking anywhere anytime soon.

"Does it hurt when I do this?" I asked him a few times. He answered yes to everything. The only thing that I could do to help him was wrap it and make sure he barely moved it.

There was nothing around that I could use as a bandage to wrap Ren's ankle in, and I wasn't wearing an undershirt, but Paul had to be wearing one as usual.

"Give me a shirt," I said. Saying please to him was a rarity for me, which started about three weeks after we had met each other.

"What? No," he spat. "This is my best one."

"I was talking about your undershirt."

"I was too!"

"Ahhhh!" Ren screamed, probably just so Paul would shut up, and maybe so I would too.

"Fine," Paul mumbled, ripping off his jacket and shirts. I always forgot how buff he was, but this was most certainly not the time to be admiring that. I mean...that is if Ren wasn't here and screaming his vocal chords to shreds. "Bugger. Here!"

He threw me his sweaty white wife beater as every drop of his attraction melted away. Ew.

"Thanks." I immediately ripped it from the neck down before Paul either looked like he was about to faint or murder me, but probably both.

"The bloody hell did you need to do that for?"

"You expect me to wrap this entire thing around his puny little ankle?"

Ren gave me a look that said, "Would you two just shut up already?" But then I noticed the sweat dripping from his forehead. Oh boy, the pain was starting to get to him.

After I finished wrapping his foot, there was nothing but silence between the three of us for at least ten minutes. Nobody knew what to say, and I'm pretty sure Ren still thought this was either a prank or a dream.

"Right," said Paul, collapsing to the ground. "Let's all just rest for a bit, fam." He probably didn't wanna admit it, but he was getting hella tired. He was right, though. It had been a long freaking night, and I was expecting to be in bed hours ago. Many, many hours ago.

I would have loved to know what time it was, but it was the twenty-first century, and all of us were cheap fucks that didn't wear watches. Besides, those probably would have just broken too like everything else.

"Who did this to us?" I mumbled, trying to think of a different pointless question to ask.

"John," Ren managed to get out. "He had to be involved. What was it that he said about this job?"

We all did the thing where we tilted our heads back and closed our eyes.

"The wife couldn't know," I said.

"This guy, Samuel, wanted to sell an antique chair," Paul added.

"John didn't know his last name," Ren continued, accusing John. "He said, and I quote, 'Samuel Something'. We all thought he could have just been growing careless, but he was involved."

"But why?" Paul defensively asked. "What could possibly be in this for him? We just had our best gig yet, and he's too smart for this."

"What do you mean?" I asked him. Not that I disagreed with him. John was a genius. At...well everything and anything that I could think of. I'd say he was probably even smarter than Ren.

"John knew we would be down here, right? He knew this was some kind of a sick job. He knew we would get out and strangle the wretched life out of him. It was a trick after all. This has to be some sort of trap. He just put a target on his back and on his forehead at the same time."

The way *target* and *back* dripped so easily from his lips concerned me. I'd never seen him this angry.

"We're not killers," I said, defending ourselves. But he wasn't listening. A realization overcame him as his eyebrows sprouted to his forehead lines. I was so not excited to listen to whatever this was gonna be. "What?"

"Unless…" He almost seemed too afraid to finish.

"WHAT?"

"Unless he didn't mean for us to escape." I could feel Ren's anger on my shoulder that was closest to him. The feeling seeped into my veins and went straight to my head. If the light was any better, they would be able to see the red in my face and eyes.

"No," I quietly whispered. "That's not what's gonna happen. We are not gonna die."

"We don't even know what this place is yet," Ren added. "We just gotta get through this tunnel. It's us. We can figure it out."

Ren's voice sounded so rusty and achy, I shushed him to stop talking. He was gonna need save as much energy as he could, and the heat in here wasn't gonna help.

"Why do I have a little twitch that's telling me it's gonna be a hell of a lot more complicated than that?" Paul asked.

"I don't know," I responded, pulling my face down with my hands. "But for now, we just gotta wait a little before Ren can walk, or even move." Paul could probably tell that I wasn't hopeful or optimistic in anything that I was saying. He was always smart in that way. He could read people better than any human being that I'd ever met. "Look. I am getting just as antsy as you. If I can be patient. So can you."

Paul shrugged before he defensively spread his arms out and said, "Fine."

"You said so yourself. Let's just rest for a sec. Try and get some sleep."

He smacked his back to the cave's wall and slid down into the most lethargic position I'd ever seen him in. It didn't look comfortable in the slightest. But as usual, he didn't say a goddamn thing back to me.

5:
REN

The pain was slowly decreasing, but not enough for me to move it let alone walk or limp on it. Numbness was the goal, but how was I to reach that with nothing surrounding me but rocks or whatever this tunnel was made of? I highly doubted there was a first aid kit anywhere hidden in here or a fridge with ice.

"I can carry you," said Paul. It would have been a kind gesture if it sounded more like an offer and less like a boasting threat.

"But for how long?" I asked. Paul didn't go to the gym *that* often. Sure, I may never have grown past five foot seven, but as my doctor liked to say, "I was plump but still springy for my height."

"I don't know, but can we just try, mate? I'm not too knackered anymore. I have the energy. We need to get moving."

"Why?" Chess shouted. "There's no point. The end of the tunnel is nowhere near us. We have made zero progress. We could just keep hurting ourselves. Maybe that's the trap or something. So, what's the goddamn point?"

I think she might have said something else, but my stomach started growling so loudly that it became a reasonable distraction.

"We need to eat something eventually," I said. "We've been walking for hours."

"Do you see any Dunkin Donuts around?" Paul snapped. "Because, I don't think that's happening anytime soon, Ren."

Instead of defending me, Chess just rolled her eyes as she re-tightened the bandage on my foot. I tried not to over think it or take it personal. We were all getting irritable, which is why I had to ignore them and look away only for a moment.

"Why don't we both carry him?" Chess suggested. "He can just hop on one leg."

"Ugh..." Paul moaned, probably rolling his eyes. Sometimes, I couldn't comprehend him. Every once in a while, I felt the urge to dissect his behavior and understand what was happening in that giant head of his. However, he sucked up his pride and apparently his testicles before he said, "Fine."

This was going to be fun. The last time I hurt this ankle, it was their fault too. We were running away from a client that we stole from, but it was Paul's fault. He had let slip that we worked for someone this client knew to be a thief. Chess didn't bother to cover up. As usual, she only wanted to be done and leave. We rarely told the truth to any human being we met after that.

"Alright, welp. Up, up, up," said Chess in her automated nurse voice.

Paul, of course, didn't help with this part, but Chess grabbed me from under my arms, and told me to put all of my weight onto one foot. Oddly enough, it took me a second to understand what the hell she was talking about, and I straightened up to balance on one leg. I could physically feel her ego overflowing as she acknowledged her ability to pick me up all by herself. She often bragged about her kung fu and boxing skills.

"Ahhh," I huffed, the moment I tried to keep my legs straight. Blood rushed to my lower body. It was almost as if melting wax dripped down my legs. "I don't know if I can do this."

"You'll be fine, mate," Paul immediately snapped the second I finished my sentence. But when both of my legs went numb and my entire body felt faint, I unintentionally proved him wrong by...well...fainting.

"Hold up, hold up," I think Chess muttered repeatedly as she caught me and lowered me back to the floor. Paul probably helped a little bit but I couldn't tell. "We need to stay here for just a little longer. He needs to elevate his foot, and the pain needs to decrease or else he's not gonna be able to tolerate it."

"Yeah, yeah. Fine," said Paul.

Chess laid me down flat on the ground and held my foot on her lap. Nothing was progressing. Not my pain, not this journey, and definitely not our safety. Who knew what could be in here? And besides, that light at the end of the tunnel was getting no larger. Not a spec of hope surrounded us.

"I'm sorry," I stumbled. "You guys go ahead. I'm not going anywhere."

"Yeah right," said Paul, surprisingly. "We've always protected each other. We're not gonna come to a halt now."

"Protected from what?" Chess spat. "We've barely completed any dangerous jobs. What are you talking about?" I could tell Chess was just trying to be brave. As the only woman in this group, there were without a doubt countless times where she felt uncomfortable. Creepy, manipulative men were everywhere. She never wanted to say anything. Vulnerability was her kryptonite after all. But I could always see it in her eyes after a job. If an older, invasive man ever came near her, her guard would immediately go up, and it would stay there for a while.

"Some of the things that we do are risky, alright? That's what I'm talking about."

I could barely pay attention to what they were saying. It wasn't precisely the pain that overwhelmed me at this point, but the pressure made my ankle feel like it was about to explode, and I could do nothing but breathe like a chihuahua.

"Why don't you go ahead?" Chess suggested to Paul. "Explore. See if there's anything you can find or just keep walking."

"I doubt it," Paul responded. "Maybe I should walk back. See if there's anything that we missed."

"I really think that's just gonna be a waste of time."

"How do you know that?"

"I don't. You're just getting on my last nerve, and I'm surprised I even have this much patience to have this conversation with you."

If Paul had any hair, he probably would have dramatically brushed it out of his face and lusciously brushed his fingers through it. It's not that he hated being told what to do or being given suggestions by a woman, but when he thought something was a bad idea, he had no problem letting every single human being know how he felt. Even if it was just some random person on the street. That's how strong his urge would be.

"Fine. If anything happens, I'll just scream."

"Hopefully we'll still be able to hear you," I joked. Actually, I might have been serious, but I wasn't going to tell him that.

"If it's anything that crawls, you'll be able to hear me." I didn't think it was possible, but as he walked away, he sank deeper into the darkness, almost as if he were invisible.

"Please tell me it's starting to feel better," said Chess without her latest consoling voice.

"Maybe. I don't know. I'm trying not to think about it."

"Good. Maybe it'll heal faster."

After I could no longer hear Paul's footsteps, the brutal silence discomforted me to no end. At least when we were walking for the past few hours, the sounds of our shoes kicking the rocks sharpened our sense of hearing, and kept ourselves attentive.

"Can you just talk to me a little?" I asked Chess. "This place is starting to creep me out even more now. Who knew that was possible - hah."

But before she could even show emotion that would predict her answer, somebody got to talking first.

"*Stiiiick,*" I heard somebody whisper as if they were right behind me and sensually whispering into my ear. It almost echoed as the voice quietly repeated the incantation a few more times. "*Stick, stick, stiiiick.*"

"AHHH!" I hollered, backing up and letting my leg fall out of Chess's care. My fright scared me to the point where I didn't even notice if any pain struck me.

"What? What?" Chess looked like I just dropped a baby. "What is it? What's wrong?"

"You didn't hear that?"

"Hear what?" How did she not hear that? It was as clear as day. The voice sounded like a dying frog, but the enunciation was flawless. I heard exactly what they said. Whoever it was.

"Somebody -" I knew we were stuck in a peculiar cave with no answer of how we got here or how we were supposed to get out, but this was about to make me sound, as Paul would say it, *bonkers*. "I heard someone whisper directly in my ear."

"Ren, there's no one here. I sure as hell didn't whisper anything to you."

"Are you sure?" She didn't look at me like I was crazy. Instead she looked at me like I was a thirteen-year-old girl looking at herself in the mirror and calling herself fat. "I can see well enough to tell you that there is no one behind you, and there never was."

Suddenly, we heard shoes slapping against the floor, running our way.

"What happened?" Paul shouted, a little out of breath. "What's wrong? Is everything okay? I heard yelling."

"I heard somebody whisper the word 'stick' into my ear. I swear to you it's true. I'm not making it up. It was like they were right behind me, but nobody was. It was a woman's voice. A crystal-clear woman's voice, and it was...loud."

Paul believed me. I could tell. As anyone could guess, if he didn't believe me, he would make it obvious and tell me to stop being such a wanker or just laugh uncontrollably. No. Instead, he looked around as if he was convinced the whisperer was still somewhere around us. I never took Paul to be a superstitious person, but he probably still thought this was all some maniacal prank with pulleys and booby traps.

"Are you okay?" He asked me for probably the first time ever.

"I'm fine. It just freaked me out. It was like those A.S.M.R. videos but worse somehow."

I felt like I should have had a cup of soup and a blanket wrapped around me. I hated being seen as weak, but at least they were acting like they cared.

"Did you hear it?" he asked Chess.

Chess probably felt bad answering. Sometimes she could surprisingly be a little compassionate. She shook her head as if she was extremely disappointed and didn't want to let me down.

"He was really freaked out though," she tried to convince him.

"I know. I could hear."

"He'll be fine. Just keep going. We'll catch up with you."

Paul was even more hesitant than before. Let's hope he didn't have a weird thing about people whispering into his ear. He would faint like a nervous cartoon character getting a flu shot.

"It's fine," I told him.

He pierced his slightly glowing eyes into mine and asked, "But what do you think that means?"

"Does it look like I know?" He wasn't used to seeing me defending myself like that. Usually I just kept quiet, but my foot was probably the size of a football right now. (I was too

28

squeamish to look.) The last thing that I cared about was Paul's tough-guy ego.

"Alright, mate. Geez. I'll just - go."

Both Chess and I nodded our heads not knowing what else to say or do. Paul was probably so confused. The only reason I say that is because I sure as hell was. What *was* that? And what did it have to do with anything in the cave?

Stick. Only one word and definitely not threatening. At least, so far it wasn't, in our current situation.

"You believe me, don't you?" I asked Chess.

"I don't know, but Paul definitely does. He's just too much of a wuss to admit it."

6:
PAUL

I hated this. I hated walking alone. The only sense of comfort that I had was knowing that Chess and Ren were somewhere behind me. Therefore, if something bonkers came strolling down the tunnel, it would run into them first and maybe more screaming would give me some sort of warning. Maybe I was too far this time, but maybe not. If anything, I had to keep my eyes as bug wide as they could go, and continue staring at the small light ahead of me.

For at least ten straight minutes, I couldn't stop thinking about what Ren heard, or felt, or whatever it was. He was certain it was a whisper, a clear and crisp whisper as he wouldn't let us forget.

Stick, I kept repeating to myself over and over. Definitely not as intimidating or scary as "Redrum," unless of course this bugger was talking about sticking something up your ass. That would be another story.

The part that made me want to hide in my jumper, however, was Ren's assurance that the whisper was as close to his ear as one could get. That's nightmare shit right there. That's the part where you jump straight up, sweating like a pig, recovering from your dream. I couldn't imagine how that must have felt being awake. But what the bloody hell did it mean? And why couldn't Chess hear it too? Would I have been able to hear it?

I prayed this wasn't meant to be some sick joke that John was playing at us. It wasn't John's style, or at least I didn't think it was. Honestly, none of us really knew him that well, but we always thought we did because he knew *us* so well. Which made perfect sense. Even Ren sometimes had trouble shutting up.

The walk was now just plain boring. The shivering fear had lowered a tad, but now all my attention was driving toward my sore hip, which bothered me when I walked too much at one time. Maybe it was just from aging, but I knew damn certain that I wasn't going to be able to run if I needed to. I was gonna need another stupid break soon, but I carried on for the moment nonetheless. For now, I could keep pushing.

Stick...stick...stick...No, stop! Forcing myself to stop thinking about it was gonna be one of the more difficult tasks on this journey. My OCD didn't let me ignore things easily. But I preferred thinking about what I was gonna do to John's face after we got out of here. That was of course if -

BANG!

Pathetically, it took me a moment to realize that it was my face that made that noise as it hit something right in front of me. The tunnel still wasn't bright, but there was nothing in front of me. I would think running into one of those stones that looked like they were icicles melting from the top of the cave would be normal, but there was nothing there. I did all of the usual things; rub my eyes, blink a thousand and one times. But nothing. There was absolutely nothing. However, I played the noise in my head over a few times just to make sure I wasn't hallucinating or being an idiot. To me, it almost sounded like I hit...glass? Like the sound you make when knocking on a glass window or door.

Oh shit. No way.

An idea struck me. A stupid, impossible, ridiculous idea. There was no way. Was there? I didn't wanna do the whole dramatic reach out by the hand just to be shocked or tackled or something stupid. Instead I held out my fist, took a step forward, and knocked on an invisible wall.

"The bloody hell did this come from?"

I was stuck. I could go back, but what good was that gonna do? I sure as hell wasn't gonna wait for those two wankers to catch up to me, which was originally our plan, but right then my patience was lower than Chess's daily dose was.

My hands slid all the way across the entire wall. The glass was so smooth, it would have made a great toy for children and Ren to slide across. No openings, at least not on my level. The top of the tunnel did reach around twelve feet tall. I certainly wasn't jumping up that high.

Maybe it was breakable. Yes, of course. How stupid of me.

About ten yards away, I brushed my trainers back like a horse getting ready to win the race. After a deep dramatic stare at an invisible wall, I charged at it like Superman breaking through the earth's ozone layer. But unlike Superman, I didn't even make a crack as I almost tripped on my way to running into the wall and falling onto the floor, shoulder first. Cheeky.

"Dammit!"

One last thought ran through my head as I glanced over to where the tunnel met the invisible glass. The only thing I could do was to dig out the wall. That was, if these rocks on the side of the cave were even removable. Well...I had to try.

With one barely working arm, I pulled myself over to the side of the tunnel. But before I could say that I made the three-yard walk over gracefully, I managed to, once again, fall over. Only this time, I was wishing I'd run into the bloody invisible wall again.

"GOD - MOTHER!" I screamed as I tripped and fell onto a family of rocks, flat on my back, and probably scraped up my almost good hand. "Jesus."

Before thinking of anything else, I immediately wiggled my knees and toes, just to make sure my back wasn't broken. I'd never been so happy to feel the sweat shake off my legs as they joggled around.

I was fine, but a painful fine. There were no more ideas in my head, but I had to get up. I was gonna be nothing but sore as a dog if I didn't, but as I pulled my almost good hand off the small rock, I noticed a sort of resistance on my skin. Like there was some sort of sticky slime. There wasn't enough light to see what it was, but the second I pulled all five fingers to my face I cracked a wise ass smile and whispered, "*Stick*."

I got it, or at least I thought I did. But what else could it have been? I've never believed in coincidences so I pulled my sticky ass off the rocks that had almost crushed my tailbone, and rubbed the saliva-like mixture into my hands to the point that I wasn't entirely sure it would come off in the wash.

Temptation teased me as my curiosity wanted to know if this was honey or not, but I wasn't interested in getting poisoned, so I just let it slide.

Just for extra precaution, my trainers trotted across the sticky rocks to assist in my climb. Bugger, this could have been even more embarrassing than the failed collision into the wall.

After staring at the ceiling, praying that I wasn't gonna fall and crack my head open, I reached my right hand straight above my head and stuck that gorilla glue honey straight onto the invisible glass like a child tracing their hand to make a Thanksgiving turkey drawing.

"I need to find a new job," I whispered.

Like climbing a ladder, my left foot naturally brought me to a climbing position. I tried to pull my right hand away, but it wouldn't budge. Neither would my foot. It was almost as if this honey stuff was specifically meant for this wall. Like peanut butter and chocolate.

Alright, time to pull yourself up, I thought. *This better work.*

Too bad my football team wasn't here. Or at least some American cheerleaders would have been nice.

"Ready?" I said to myself. "Three, two -" And just like Chess would have done, I lost my patience too quickly to finish that sentence and made a single crawl up the wall. "Well, I'll be damned."

One foot after the other, but it came at a price. This shit was less like honey and more like glue. My skin felt as if it was gonna rip from my bones every time I peeled my rough hands off the smooth glass, but so far, no blood. Thank the lord. Between blood and heights, I would have passed out right then and there but left hanging with my hands stuck to a wall that nobody could see. Chess and Ren would have been quite puzzled.

Only a few feet left. I doubt I would have been able to compare myself to Spiderman just yet, but maybe more like a disheveled spider that had lost four of its legs.

The glue was losing its grip, but I was close to the top. I only hoped there was an opening. Surprisingly, my ears started to pop. Yawning wasn't doing much, but I wouldn't let it distract me. Just a few more inches. If there was an opening, there would be just enough room for me to squeeze my broad shoulders and hips through it. At least some blood would surely spill, or perhaps more like splatter all over my body. Those rocks looked sharp as hell.

Naturally, I could feel my fingers clench together as if they were trying to squeeze the juice out of an orange. My shaky feet couldn't help but feel like they were about to slip at any moment.

Come on, come on.

Sometimes I had to remind myself that I needed no one's encouragement but my own. At least most of the time I didn't. But staring straight ahead, holding onto nothing but invisible glass, and being quite a few yards in the air, my confidence wasn't at its best. Some hyping up from Chess and Ren couldn't have hurt.

"Alright, three, two, one." My mind erased for a split second while my fingers aggressively folded over the top of the thick glass. It was maybe three inches wide. No wonder I couldn't break through this thing. For a split second, my chest stopped pounding. Knowing I had a firm grip, a little chuckle slipped out with my breath. But alas, the security couldn't last for long.

Before I could pull myself up, my shoes refused to work with me anymore. The glue ripped apart between my soles and the glass. The only thing keeping me from falling was four knuckles curved over the top of the wall.

"FUCK!" I screamed as my feet slid down. Thank the Lord I'd been doing pull ups at the gym. I wasn't gonna be able to hold much longer, but my other hand slapped over the edge and fiber by fiber my thick arms pulled me over the top of the glass wall. One knee slid over the top before I could feel the rocks on the ceiling dig into my back. The farther over I got, the deeper and deeper the weapon-like stones dug into my spine and skin. Maybe I underestimated how big I was, but that wasn't the most painful part.

The limper my body was, the more the glass dug into my ribcage, stomach, and worst of all, my poor groin. There was nothing I could do. A deep, horror film-like scream needed to burst out.

"AHHHHHHH!" And with all of the air in my body escaping from my scream, I rolled over to the other side, grabbing onto the top of the glass at the last second. The longer I hung with all ten knuckles holding me up, the more I could feel the blood from my back dripping down my skin.

Only one more thing to do, or at least I was pretty sure it was the last step.

Just fall, you'll be fine, my conscience fought with me. I thought this lad was being a nutter, but for some reason, I listened to him anyway. There was no way I was waiting to crawl down.

One by one, pinky first, the fingers peeled away from the sticky shit and the glass. Well...no going back now. One hand at a time. Once again, thank God for the existence of pull ups, but, of course, I spoke too soon. Actually, in my opinion, I usually spoke just at the right time. Although, when my first hand ripped away from the glass and swung down so harshly that it almost pulled off the skin from my other hand, and the rest of my body slammed into the floor, I re-evaluated my ego. Thankfully, I landed on my feet. Otherwise, I would have had to lie to everyone including myself about this incident.

"Bugger," I mumbled as I shook out my tingling ankles, until something shook my balance, like literally *shook*. What was shaking? Honestly, I couldn't tell, or at first, I couldn't. "God please, nooo." My voice never sounded so breath-like, realizing it could only be one thing; another bloody earthquake. Whether it was coming from actual American soil or just the tunnel, I wasn't sure, but there's no way two fake earthquakes were a coincidence. Somebody had to be watching us.

So many loose rocks and sand crumbled from the ceiling, I was convinced there wasn't going to be any left. Not wanting to damage any more of my body, naturally I closed my eyes as tight as they could, but less than half a second after I did, light poked through my eyelids. I had to open them back up. What was happening? I had no clue. I had to open them. I needed to know.

A section of the floor broke off, lifting me up to the outdoors. Like in a boxing arena, presenting myself to the audience, I rose into the light, thinking I was about to escape.

Oh, Lord. I'm getting out of here, I thought, only slightly feeling guilty about leaving Ren and Chess behind. They would figure it out eventually, right?

But when my journey past the top of the rocky tunnel came to a close, disappointment and frustration shot right back up my spine and throat.

This wasn't Atlanta, this was just another tunnel, but something was...familiar. Nothing seemed different except for -

"The light," I whispered. The single light at the end of the tunnel. It was bigger. Quite bigger, actually.

7:
CHESS

Vrooooooooooo BOOOOOM!

That's all I heard, but barely. Something was wrong. I could feel it.

"What was that?" Ren asked, barely awake.

"Does it look like I know?" I snapped for no reason. I didn't hear Paul scream, but I wasn't sure if that was a good or a bad thing.

"Paul?" I called out knowing damn well he wasn't gonna answer. I turned back to Ren knowing he wasn't gonna like what I was about to say. "I'm gonna go see what's up."

"What?" I could have sworn he was gonna grab onto my ankle as I tried to leave. "You're just going to leave me here?"

"Look." I didn't remember the last time I lost my patience with him this much. Something about his vulnerability irritated me to no end. "If someone wanted to hurt us, they would have done it by now, and if someone else was here, they would have let us know by now. Okay? I know you're not gonna go anywhere, but stay put."

Ren didn't say anything else. At least not full words. It was more like, "Ah - uh - buh?" But without hesitation, I popped up and walked my way down the tunnel.

Walking down there alone felt empowering. I guess it was because I couldn't let myself be afraid. There was no time for it, and it was gonna do nothing but slow me down. Speaking of slowing down, I felt a sudden urge to go just a hair faster, but as my feet sped up, I couldn't resist. I needed to *run*.

My sweat broke almost immediately, and with the heat beaming off my face, my speed progressively grew to its peak. Nothing was going to hurt me here, especially not my claustrophobia.

The time dragged on like a soap opera as I kept pushing my feet to go faster and faster. But as sweat continued to fly off my nose more and more frequently, my vision began to blur. What if I already passed him? Somebody could have tucked him away in a corner too, or some*thing*.

"Paul?" I screamed out. "Paul, what was that? Where are you?" No answer. Not even a whisper, or the sound of a rock being kicked. Just silence. More running, I guess.

The chaffing under my arms hated me more than any of my ex-boyfriends or clients that I ripped off. And without any food or water in my body, I wasn't sure how much longer I was gonna last. With the ache in my throat, and pain in my stomach, my body forced me to walk like it was pushing my soul out of me, but at least I was still able to move forward.

"Chess? Ren?" I faintly heard Paul's voice. Funny, it almost sounded like it was coming from above.

"Paul? Where are you? What happened?"

"I'm up here!" But I couldn't see him. He sounded like the principal speaking over an intercom but with an old broken mic.

"Where? What do you mean 'here'?" I knew he wasn't in the tunnel anymore, but my dumbass still whipped my head and shoulders frantically from side to side.

"I'm above the cave. Well, I'm still in the tunnel, I guess just on another level. I think this place acts like a staircase, but we have to pass the riddle or something." Riddle? What kind of game was John playing? Why did he set us up with this job?

"You're kidding right?" I asked.

"I was just raised above an endless tunnel by a magical floor and you're asking me if I'm kidding?" I didn't say anything back. Rude. "Is the wall still there?"

"Wall? What wall? The cave walls have been here the whole time."

"No, no. The -" His hesitance implied he had something ridiculous to tell me. Damn, this oughta be good. "The invisible wall. Is it still there? Do you feel it?" Well, would ya look at that? Spot on.

"Jesus, an invisible wall?"

"JUST LOOK! IT'S THE ONLY WAY YOU CAN GET UP HERE!" Paul already had an intense, booming voice. Trust me, raising his voice was beyond unnecessary, but try telling him that.

"Alright, alright, fine I'll -" Welp, found it. "Ow, I hit my nose. Is this shit glass?" Instead of answering, I only heard the faintest chuckle coming from right above my head. Asswipe. "Oh, shut up. What do I have to do?"

"Rub your hands and feet on the sticky stuff that's all around the rocks right next to you. Remember 'stick'? It was a clue. Whoever the woman was, she was giving us a clue." I wanted to be happy he figured out what the hell this whisper thing was, but I couldn't think about it.

Uh oh...sticky stuff?

"It's just on the rocks?" I asked him.

"Yeah, it'll help you climb over the wall."

"Right. It's not honey though, is it?"

"Honey doesn't stick that much, but it might have it in the mixture or whatever these fuckfaces wanna call it, why?"

"I'm allergic to honey. Deathly allergic." Silence. If I wasn't gonna be able to climb over that wall, they would have to leave me behind.

"When the ceiling opens, I will be here to grab you, and we can figure it out." Figure it out? Solid plan, but what else was he supposed to say? We'll go to the nearest Walgreens and get some Benadryl? Don't think so.

"Alright, I gotta go get Ren." Maybe my senses were deceiving me, but I thought I could almost hear a sigh from Paul, like it was a severe inconvenience for him.

"Yeah. Right. Go."

Quickly, my mind had the unreasonable urge to convince me that if I kept my heart rate going, I wouldn't have an allergic reaction. Being a retired nurse, I knew that wasn't quite how it worked, but still. Don't get me wrong, I wouldn't have to eat it or anything, but skin contact usually resulted in breathing trouble and thick hives that could last for days. The only choice that I had was to cross my fingers and see.

The light jog back to Ren didn't pull me away from reality as much as it could have. I wouldn't let it. For a brief moment, just half a second, I almost thought I passed him. That was, of course, until -

"AH!" I yelled, tripping over what I realized afterwards, was his foot, but something was off. Something was terribly, frighteningly off. There was no vocal reaction to me falling over his broken foot. "Ren?" No answer. "REN?" Again, no response.

Jesus, not now. My panic led me to shake him harder than I wanted to. But hey, it worked.

"Wha-?" He mumbled.

"Jesus, don't scare me like that. Come on, get up!"

"Wait, I can do it myself." Now I was even more worried. Maybe I should've slapped him.

"As in get up?"

"Yeah, and I'll only need a little help walking. I promise, it feels better. Don't worry about me. I can do it."

I wanted to argue. As a nurse, everything was telling me *aw hell no*, but I was getting impatient and I was deathly afraid we were gonna run out of time. I wasn't sure why or how we would, but there was no way time was on our side.

"Alright let's go." He was right. It only took a little grunt for him to slide up onto one foot, and with deep, heavy breaths, he pushed through his first few crooked steps. For real, I got nervous he was gonna run away from me. "I gotcha, I gotcha. Come on, we gotta be quick."

My anxiety not only went through the roof, it basically blasted the roof to shreds. With every breath I had I kept trying to keep the pace while Ren gradually slowed down, but we were almost there. Almost to the next step. Literally.

I filled Ren in on the way, but I doubt he caught onto anything. That kid was brilliant, but his sweat didn't stop sprinkling all over me the whole walk over there. He wouldn't be concentrating on shit anytime soon.

"Almost there," I told him.

"Chess? Ren?" Paul shouted out as we got closer. "Ren, you doing okay, mate?"

"I'm fine."

"Can you climb?"

"Yeah, I'll figure it out." Wow, that was reassuring and enthusiastic. But nonetheless, we hobbled over to the rocks with the sticky shit spread all over them. "You okay?"

I wasn't sure how to answer that, but I was never sure how to answer that question regardless of the situation. Looking weak or difficult was never something that I enjoyed admitting to.

"Yeah. Come on. It's gotta go all over the bottom of our shoes and hands." My spread-out fingers came an inch from the rocks. Just to check, I held them there. Only for a moment to see if I could feel a tingle. Not that it would tell me anything, but when I finally came to terms with the fact that I had no choice, I aggressively rubbed my hands deep into the substance until the skin on my hands couldn't breathe. "We need to do this quickly, okay?" I wasn't sure what he said to me in return. I couldn't hear over the sound of my heart beating out of my chest. Or more like popping out and sucking back in. The scary part was the fact that I didn't know if it was beating like that because I was nervous or if it was the beginning of a dangerous allergic reaction.

"Ready?" Ren asked me as if we were beginning a race.

"Let's go." And like the genius that he is, Ren slapped both hands as far up as they could reach then gently slapped his bad foot against the invisible wall and began to climb. Slowly, but surely.

A minute later I thought, *A few feet away from the top now*. It took a second for me to notice that I'd been holding my breath for a while. But when I tried to take a secure, deep breath, that was when my heart went from popping, to full stop. I couldn't breathe. I mean I could, but it was like a hiccup breath; tiny and almost painful.

Shit, shit, shit, I said in my head over and over again until I couldn't think anymore. I was almost there, but what was I gonna do? And who made this stuff? What sick asshole thinks of a booby trap like this?

Almost there. My entire elbow folded over the top, and my knee was able to swing over and latch on. I couldn't even look to see if Ren was still climbing, but my head was basically numb anyways when I was finally able to swing my entire body over the ledge. So numb that I couldn't hold myself up anymore, and with limp arms and legs, I fell straight down and plunged into the tunnel floor.

"Chess? Ren? What was that?" I could hear Paul holler, not being able to see what was going on, but I couldn't respond. No matter how hard I tried, I could barely move any part of my body. However, that unfortunately didn't mean I couldn't *feel*. Whatever was in that substance, there was definitely a hell of a lot of honey, because I didn't need to look at my skin to know it had hives all over it.

"AHH" I heard, which was probably Ren falling even more ungracefully than I had done. At least it must have been Ren, because all I could see for the next few seconds were rocks falling every which way around me and the ground, slowly but quickly at the same time, lifted Ren and I to meet Paul on the next level of the tunnel.

It was like a mixture between an earthquake and one of those massage tables that vibrated. Nothing about it was scary, but that was only because I was, you could say, a bit distracted that I was gonna suffocate before fear instilled in me.

"Chess! CHESS!" One of the boys said. I wasn't sure which one. Was this what being in a coma was like?

"I - I -" I tried to tell them that I was alive and that consciousness was seeping back into me. Nothing like sobering up in a dark cave with obnoxious, sweaty, and somewhat bloody men crowding around me. "I - I'm fine. I can breathe." Damn maybe I was telling the truth for once since my fingers could wiggle like they were playing the guitar. Painfully, but they were coming back to life faster than they usually did when I had an allergic reaction. "Pull me up," I told them without saying please, like usual.

"You sure you can?" Ren asked literally as he was, in fact, helping me to stand, with his bad foot.

"Yes! I said I'll be fine. At least I can walk." Ren was not impressed, but what was he gonna do? Run away? "Let's just go, okay?"

I took Ren's arm and we started to, what most people wouldn't call "walk," but it was close enough. However, after taking a few steps I noticed that I didn't hear a third set of footsteps.

"Paul?" I called out before I turned around and saw him standing lifeless. For all I knew he could have just been electrocuted. "Paul?" I asked a few more times until he finally answered with barely even a lip quiver.

"I - I just heard the next clue," he said.

"What?" Ren shouted out before I could. "What is it?"

"*Shock*."

8:
PAUL

"How's that foot, mate?" I repeatedly asked Ren only to annoy him. He kept responding with either a mumble, which apparently meant "stop asking," or a thumbs up. Painfully, we moved slower than a snail, but we were moving in general, and Ren was surprisingly being quite the champ about it. Chess reminded him to breathe over and over again, which probably annoyed him more than me. Looked like there was about to be a little competition between us. Honestly, I really did sometimes take too much pride in my ability to annoy Ren, and pretty much every other human being that I interacted with.

Anyway, Ren would probably be the last person to forget to breathe. If it was the norm to set timers as reminders to breathe, he would absolutely set them, just to be organized.

"You okay over there?" Chess asked before it took me a second to realize she was talking to me.

"What? Oh, yeah. I'm good. It's still all just strange." I didn't usually mind showing fear. That only made boasting of conquering it all the more fun, but being this creeped out was awkward to talk about. Most parents and teachers were not equipped with telling their children how to talk about traumatic experiences in supernatural caves.

"Ain't that the truth? I'm just not excited to figure out what the fuck 'shock' could mean."

"You want me to take him for a while?" I asked, trying to change the subject. After being in the army and knowing what a taser felt like, I wasn't too excited to figure out if the clue was literal or mental.

"Sure. I'm pretty sure he's asleep anyway."

"Shut up," Ren snapped out of the blue. There's the annoyance I was looking for. Beautiful. He wrapped his small arm up and around my shoulder since he was too short to fully reach across it. "How long have we been walking?"

"About a half an hour," Chess responded with a slight sigh in her voice. "Or probably around a half an hour."

It took absolutely everything in me not to respond with some sort of snarky comment like, "Hm, I'm shocked you were

42

paying attention. Damn! Maybe that's what the clue means; We're all shocked Chess isn't being completely dramatic. Bring us to the next level!" But I didn't. I was in a cheekier mood than usual.

"You know what I could go for right about now?" I asked everyone, knowing they weren't gonna care ahead of time.

"Wha-?" They both mumbled.

"A juicy, American, bacon egg and cheese from MacDonald's."

"Oh, don't tease us, asshole," Chess spat. "Although I would love a McFlurry to go along with that."

It was all good reminiscing until Ren ruined the moment and said in his fake, deep voice, "I'd rip that McFlurry right out of your hand to hold it up to my goddamn foot."

"Fine. Then, I'd just make you buy me another one." Something that Chess would absolutely do.

It was, indeed, the oddest thing...we laughed. We literally laughed in response. All three of us. Usually when we laughed, it was because we just managed to rip off some idiot, and it was gonna take them at least a day to figure it out.

Strange. Ren's laugh almost sounded like purring. Either that or it was his stomach growling. Even stranger, it didn't stop.

"Does anyone hear that?" Ren asked.

"Mate," I nervously laughed. "I thought that was your stomach."

"No. Is it yours, Chess?"

She shook her head, not knowing what the hell we were talking about. She always was a deaf little bugger.

It wasn't the sound that made me stop in my tracks, per se, but rather the increasing volume that made my jaw tighten like I'd just seen a terrorist attack. Or it could have been the glowing eyes that grew bigger and deeper as they bounced closer to us.

"You've got to be kidding me," Chess whispered. Creeping out of the dark, stepping one paw in front of the other, stood a drooling tiger with the brightest orange and white strips. Something was around its neck, but I was too worried about my life flashing before my eyes and the visions of being mercilessly eaten alive.

"What do we do? What do we do?" Ren almost certainly kept saying that same sentence over and over again. But who would pay attention to a single syllable coming out of that dweeb's mouth when a full-grown tiger is crawling toward you with hunting, prowling eyes, at almost two meters away?

"We can't run," Chess added as softly as she possibly could. "It'll just chase us."

"Slowly," I said. "Very slowly, just crouch down and cover your head. Don't make eye contact with it." Every single one of our beating hearts synchronized. I knew because I could easily hear them all. It wasn't hard.

The bright, almost heroic-looking tiger kept their paws rolling toward us. Slowly, but with a crystal-clear purpose. The tiger's round pendant dangled on its collar-like, silver necklace. The color of the circle perfectly matched the color of the reddish-brown rocks surrounding us, but I didn't have time to wonder why the hell a tiger would be wearing a kitty-cat collar, let alone why it would be bare and tasteless. With submissive attitudes we mocked its behavior; careful and silent. Yet we had the courtesy of not licking our lips in return.

Closing my eyes was somehow the first and last thing that I wanted to do. My feet almost lost their balance while I ungracefully but silently crouched into a ball. Naturally, I closed my eyes and let them merge with my knees.

Maybe it was the lack of air in my brain and lungs, but from my point of view, no one was making a sound. Ren wasn't whistling through his nose like he usually did, and Chess wasn't whimpering as she always did when she was doing something that she didn't wanna do. But best of all, I couldn't hear the tiger. No sand crunching through the beast's toes. No growling for hunger. Maybe it was gone, but it couldn't be that easy. Could it? Even Ren was picking up on the social cues of how this tunnel worked. Wherever the tiger went, she was coming back, and soon.

Just a few more seconds, I thought. *Give it a few more seconds just to be safe.* And I did. We all did, but when I whispered "It's okay," to everyone and uncrushed my eyes from my knees, my spine unfolded, my chin tilted up, and there before me stood the brightest colored tiger I'd ever seen inches away from my face staring through my soul and into my flesh.

44

"AHHHHHH!" I stupidly screamed instantly, and impulsively. The biggest mistake I'd made so far on this so-called journey. That was it. Before I could even jump back, the tiger left no mercy or hesitation and slashed her claws deep into my shoulder. The darkness didn't even bother to cover my eyes from the blood splashing across the side of Chess's pale face.

"PAUL!" she screeched. But before she even finished my one syllable name, a hefty, red rock brushed across the animal's nose. The gravel left no physical dent, but a dent in their ego? That was negotiable.

My reactive focus snapped towards the origin of the rock's flight. There stood Ren not knowing, or probably even thinking about what to do next, but instead obsessing over his terrible aim.

"Ren! Watch out!" I hollered, but it was too late. The tiger had already leapt into the air to take a daring prance upon him. Though it was a bugger to see, something got in the way. Something that Chess sliced into the beast to weaken her.

While Ren managed to scurry back, avoiding even one claw, I could see a pocket knife sticking out of its side. The weakness oozed into the poor creature that only needed food, but maybe we could eat some food instead?

Every nerve, muscle, and fiber in her body squirmed, begging for relief, but it was only coming slower the more she moved. With what was left of her energy, the tiger swiped at Ren's ankles, but missed every time while still sprawled on her side.

"Come on, come on," Chess spoke with her most demonic eyes, staring the creature down, begging for its death and her own safety.

For the time it took for me to catch my breath, the tiger went from swiping to swaying, like it was drunkenly swatting a fly. My abnormal love for animals almost brought sympathy to my heart and soul as the movement descended from minimal to none. Not even a twitch. The poor bugger.

Of course, all that sympathy died down completely once my eyes caught sight of the strangest and most inconvenient thing; the knife, it slipped. The freaking thing slipped all on its own out of the tiger. The red spots of blood trickled on the floor with little sparkles of light in them. Like a river, but that river flooded back to its original home. Back into the body of a paranormal tiger. And after every drop of the stream seeped past the fur, the cut sewed itself back together, with nothing but magic or voodoo or whatever the hell was poisoning this place.

"Oh, you've gotta be kidding meeeee!" Chess screamed at the bottom of her lungs, showing off the raspiness in her voice. She lunged for her knife, but the tiger got to it first. I never thought I would see the day where a giant cat would suddenly and aggressively brush away a weapon with their unopposable thumb. I'd never seen Chess so afraid, but I'd never seen her striving with so much power. No matter what would happen, Chess would never even let an animal hurt her pride, or sprinkle a sense of submission onto her. She would let people see her fear. She would tell people she was afraid, but her pride could never stand even a little chip in itself.

The tiger pounced with her arms stretched and her claws ready to slice open her prey, but Chess was quick and with the most natural movement, her head tucked and rolled to the floor. A sense of relief stung into my chest when the tiger caught her front paw under a rock, and the rest of us managed to gather up a few rocks to strike when ready.

The reborn tiger charged the second the paw slipped loose. I felt Ren's shoulder brush against mine while he flicked his weak arm and almost missed the tiger entirely.

The vibe beaming from Ren; it wasn't powerful. Not like Chess, but rather pure frustration. Like he just couldn't win.

The second or third rock that collided with the tiger's face forced its hesitation for just a moment. A special growl sprouted from her throat, until the eyes realigned with ours. Blood seeped from one of them. For however long it lasted, the giant cat was blind. Just in one eye, but of course, like I predicted when I saw the blood trickle back into its eye socket, it's like there were never any stones to begin with.

"GODDAMMIT!" I screeched. What was the word? The word - the word? The clue, idiot! What was it? Nothing in my head was functioning since apparently nothing was properly functioning out here either! Not that it should shock me at this point.

Ah, bloody hell, I thought.

"WE NEED TO FIND SOMETHING TO SHOCK IT WITH!" I screamed as loud as I could so even Chess could hear it over her ego.

"WHAT?" They both hollered back.

"LOOK FOR SOMETHING ELECTRICAL!"

Through the darkness and the stones flying one after the other, I could see Chess rolling her eyes, but I'd like to think it was just because she had to do more work than she originally thought and was not excited about it.

Scurrying across the ground, we eventually lost control of the tiger. Her smarts out-grew us. She adapted to our methods. Just the thought of that, stung my chest like a bee. We couldn't afford to take our eyes off her, or at least one eye, while using the other to find whatever electric field the woman was talking about.

The jolly, ferocious movement oozing out of that animal was intoxicating. Both in a way that was compelling and distracting. Luckily for its bright fur, we could somewhat trace the sporadic movement. The hungrier it grew, the louder and faster it became.

"REN!" I shouted, "REN! WE'LL DISTRACT IT! LOOK FOR WHATEVER'S GONNA ELECTROCUTE THIS BEAST!"

A mixture of pride and disappointment resonated within him, but he was way too smart to argue with me at this point. Although something kept clawing at me besides the thing that was *actually* clawing at me. I could dissect what was going through his brain. Maybe we were just thinking alike, but somehow, I knew he was going for Chess's knife. Smart lad.

"Over here, ya fucktard!" Chess snarled as she threw her jacket across the room, hoping the cat would chase it. Like most animals that have the attention span of a fly, it almost worked, but it gave Ren enough time to scope the middle of the cave and find the knife.

"Got it," I heard him whisper, but like the disorganized mate that he was, he stood there blank-faced like a girl just told him she fancied him.

"THROW IT SOMEWHERE, MORON!" I shouted. Pausing for pensive thoughts, I could see an idea strike into him, and with the reflexes I didn't know he had, he threw the knife into the direction we were heading towards.

Neither Chess nor I had time to think or even react to the bolt of lightning that shattered from the top, bottom, and sides of the cave, like a wall of electricity. Damn it. Not another bloody wall.

"GET IT OVER HERE!" Chess screamed. All three of us charged toward the wall creating a barrier of our own, waiting for the tiger to think she was finally gonna get her supper.

One last time, the beast snuffled its nose like it was tracking us. Taunting us. And with its marble eyes, it increased the cadence in its feet. Easy, smooth, and in a flash, quick and staccato.

"Ready?" Ren asked, as if he was the leader in this situation. But with no time to acknowledge his false sense of dominance, the beast leapt with no hesitation. And with not even a fraction of a second to spare, the three of us ducked out of the way and listened to the sound of burning flesh frying.

Even hearing the sound of death, I still hesitated to get up. We all did. But it didn't matter, we were all forced to hold onto something as we were automatically pulled up to the next level of the tunnel.

From what I could see, Paul bled from at least ten deep wounds. Five on his back from scraping against the rocks and five from each piercing claw that dug into his shoulder. That tiger had no mercy. I couldn't help but think that someone must have given him (or her, I honestly didn't notice) commands to attack us. Or maybe it was just that hungry. Whoever was testing us, they surely weren't doing it fast enough.

"Welp," said Chess as if she were about to faint. "I need to sleep."

"Thank you for being the first one to say it," I responded. Paul would have never let it down. Like always.

"Someone should take the first watch," the apparent boss suggested. Paul. In case that wasn't apparent. "I'll do it. I'm probably the least tired." Of course he was.

"No arguing with that."

Chess didn't even wait for us to finish the conversation before she dropped to the floor and slid her leather coat over her eyes. It wasn't until now that I realized how much our eyes had adjusted to the dark. We'd been creeping along this tunnel like cats or bats in the night, trying to show our dominance. Well, by the look of Paul's body (and mine, but who cares?), we could see how superbly that was going.

There was something to say. To both of them. I just couldn't think of the words. *Be careful?...Thank you for helping me?* Or maybe an obvious *Goodnight?* But the two of them despised dissecting my awkwardness when it wasn't necessary. So, it was time to simply lay my head down on a rock that felt like it was gonna slide into my skull the longer I stayed on top of it, and go. To. Sleep.

Now. Ever since I was a small kid in high school, it always took a minimum of two hours to fall asleep. Reason one: my constant anxiety. Reason two, which was the much more significant reason: my overactive brain. Unfortunately, this time my overactive brain did not save me, even though I begged it to. I was dead beat, whatever that meant. Just a few seconds. That was all it took to sink into the deepest yet haziest dream I ever had.

It was unclear as to whether or not I appreciated the fact that I immediately knew it was a dream. Although, it did take me a few brief moments to be certain that someone was putting these thoughts into me. And please, take a moment to acknowledge the fact that I said "brief." There is a difference after all.

This wasn't basic science. I knew because I understood basic science. This wasn't just a step above, this was more like a whole staircase. I'd never dreamed like I was drunk before, but then again, I've only been drunk maybe twice in my life, and one of those times was only because Paul slipped some vodka and laxatives into my drink once at a bar.

Every image in every direction dragged behind itself. The pigments pulled away like running water color on a child's painting. But even more peculiar, the colors faded in and out like fireworks flashing against human skin.

No matter how many directions I gazed upon, there were still no clues as to where the hell I was. Trees. A. Lot. Of. Trees. That was it. All I could do was just keep walking, but not voluntarily. Or maybe it was?

If I wanted to walk forward with my right foot, I would take a step to the front, but with my left foot. Manipulation varied between me and whichever asshole kept me stuck in this dream, but the fight seemed as if it was between me and myself. An odd game for sure.

The demented pathway led me to vague familiarity step by step. Not because I recognized anything yet, but just...because. Something injected through my blood and veins causing me to metaphorically open my eyes. I'd been there before. Though it was still just trees and dirt that surrounded me for what seemed like miles.

This can't be good, I thought. Being alone in the woods in any scenario could never have a positive outcome. Since when do film directors say, "We're gonna have them walk in the woods alone, but don't worry nothing bad is going to happen and everything will be totally and completely normal"? Never. That's fantasy nonsense right there.

Something materialized in the distance, like physically, literally popped out of nowhere with only a subtle, gentle pop. Like a drop of blood swirling into a pool of water.

Eagerness eased into impatience. Fatigue and confusion slid into excitement and curiosity. What was this grey, ratty, torn - Well, well. Wouldn't you know? Before me stood the house that trapped us in this godforsaken place that prevented me from eating and peeing alone. What was I doing here?

Well, no harm in going inside. This was a dream after all and it wasn't as if I could fall into the pit of despair twice.

Strange seeing this place in a twilight zone. The light gave it a completely different ring and vibe to it in a way that forced my non-negotiable attention upon it. This time, I knew no one was home. How, you ask? Whenever I have a dream, I get an alarming tingle in my toes when the dream people come near me. Usually sneaking up on me. Right now, all ten of my little piggies relaxed at ease. No one was in sight. Now, most of the time when I tell this fun fact to people, they laugh it off. A common response was, "How could you tell? Are you psychic or something?" Then I remind these idiots that dreams are not real and neither are psychics. Dreams are just figments of our imagination turned into a movie. Movies can be fairly predictable.

Creeeaaak, each step sung, only with different notes for every step. The horror soundtrack almost distracted me from noticing the note on the door with my name at the top before I walked in. Of course, every horror story requires a solid double take of the head. I just didn't expect it to come so soon. Then again, maybe I wasn't going to be asleep for much longer.

The top of the note was written in big, bold letters. Unfortunately, I wasn't able to use the excuse, *it's just a dream* in this scenario. Clown school dropouts would be able to tell you that clearly wasn't true, but as far as I knew, I couldn't be killed or physically tortured in a dream.

REN

I would hate for you to end here.
Have yourself a look around.
Maybe you'll find something useful.

51

Or maybe it will answer a few questions.
Don't disappoint me.

Of course, it wasn't signed. It was obvious who it was from. Interesting. It only made me more anxious to re-enter that demon house to prove to the others I could at least get some sort of information without them. Pessimism wouldn't dare come within ten feet of me. I had nothing to fear.

Creeeaaak.

In all honesty, I wanted to scream and say, "WE GET IT, DREAM! IT'S AN OLD CREEPY HOUSE! ENOUGH WITH THE SOUND EFFECTS!" But I figured the situation was already peculiar enough as it was.

The storm door was even heavier than I remembered. Then again, I hadn't eaten in God knows how long. Everything seemed the same, only brighter. But not brighter as if there was a significant absence of light before. Brighter as in more prominent. Each individual item perfectly placed around the living room stood out like a ballerina forgetting her sweatpants under her tutu. This wasn't a memory. Someone was forcing these images into the back of my soul and eyes.

What was I doing scattering about the room like a bunny waiting to be fed? Somebody could be giving me information, dear Lord. I eagerly needed to slow down, but the only thing I couldn't shake was if this was something that I needed to see to help *them*, or *me*?

"Hel - hel -" Damn it. Just like in every dream, especially this one, there was no running or screaming for help. You'd think with all this unnecessary technology these days, somebody would have figured out how to fix that by now. Maybe kids wouldn't taunt other children with their horror stories of how Big Bird ate them in their dream the night before. Or maybe that was just me who had that experience.

"Hello?" I finally managed to give a little holler, even though there was no point. No one was here, or at least no one was physically here. Being a man of science, I still wasn't utterly confident in what that meant.

No answer. No noise. Only unpeaceful silence. The kind of silence that forces you to turn over in your bed just to have a better visual of your entire room.

52

Alright. Just do it. Have a look around, I thought. At this point, finding something could be the only key to waking up.

Without realizing, my fingertips grazed along the antiques and walls, doing the looking for my eyes. Until something made my brow knit. I didn't want to look, but my fingers couldn't resist. They had a memory of their own, and all of my senses connected at once. Telling each other what they were feeling.

A small-ish figurine. Metal, and realistic. Keep in mind, I cradled the object with the sweaty palm of my non-dominant hand, but any idiot with the sense of touch would be able to tell you that the odd texture was undoubtedly fur. Fur, and of course, claws the size of a golf ball, which in relative proportion was considered big for this creature.

But before my gripping touch could continue, my sight had to intervene. Resisting the architects of my dream was difficult, but not impossible. I had to look back. Risking losing valuable information wasn't going to gain me credibility with Chess and Paul. A chance. That's all it was.

An unknown force pushed against my head while I fought and resisted to look back and see the face of a tiger staring straight at me. Standing maybe seven inches tall, the metal fur had the same exact vibrancy that the maniacal one did that almost tried to eat us. Behind the fur and around the neck, something else didn't bother to hide from me. The necklace, or chain, or whichever people called it these days. The real beast had one on just like it. Red with a perfectly round pendant.

What were these people doing? Making inanimate objects come to life and attack us? No. They were crazy, but not insensibly weird. No. This was inspiration for them. Inspiration for our traps. But why? Chess and Ren were going to have a field day with this.

"Wait," I whispered as if someone could hear me. If there were items in here that related to our riddles and traps before, this room could give me a clue as to what was going to come next. Even though the only way it could possibly make us more prepared was mentally. There was no stealing from this dream house, unfortunately.

Alright, I thought. *What do we have here?* But, of course, at the peak of my dream investigation, there came the most inconvenient distraction.

"*RUN, run, RUN, Ru - RUN!*" came the messy echo. Somehow it shook me less in the dream state, yet the echo sounded scattered and more random. But what the hell was she doing here in my dream?

"Wha -" I once again struggled to release the words from my mouth. "What? Where? Run where?"

Talking only made me dizzier, or maybe more controlled. Oh no, was I waking up? I couldn't. Not yet. I needed more information. More clues as to what was to terrify us next.

Come on, I told my body. Naturally, it worked to reject the request. Who tries to stay *in* a nightmare? If that's what you would call this. *Come on, Come* - but instead of finding a clue, my eye caught wind of something else. Something not useful, only cruel. A mirror. Boy I hated mirrors. Forcing me to look at the one thing that made me feel self-conscious? No, thank you. But I would take looking at a mirror any other day over this horror show. Dripping down my face was the warmest mixture of dark and bright blood. No pain. Just blood. Before I had time to inspect the scene, my own hands slapped against my face, like a reflex, causing me to wake up.

Apparently, along with my abrupt awakening, I audibly gasped for air so loudly I woke up Chess and Paul.

"Ren?" Chess mumbled with the most frog-like voice I'd ever heard come out of her.

"What's wrong, mate?" Paul asked.

Right now, there was less than zero time to answer their pathetic questions. "Guys, we have to run."

10:
CHESS

This was hopefully the only time I could ever say, "Good thing I haven't eaten anything in what's probably been a full day now!" Otherwise I would have gotten the worst runner's cramp a human could possibly imagine. I always did have a horrible digestive system, and right now, my belly button never felt so close to my spine. Although adrenaline wasn't helping. At least it wasn't yet. Nothing fearful drove us to pump our feet that fast except for the word, "Run." But it made sense as to why this step was so goddamn long.

How Paul was carrying Ren on his back and running as fast as I was, was beyond me. We looked like freaking idiots running from nothing, but still breathing a dollop of fear from our lungs.

"Does - anyone - hear - anything?" Paul asked, surprisingly annunciated for being out of breath and carrying an extra one hundred and forty pounds.

"No!" I answered quickly and efficiently. I couldn't see anything either, but running and focusing my terrible eyesight at the same time was absolutely not gonna happen.

"Chess - Chess, I need - a break!" What? Was he crazy? What if that was part of the trap that we couldn't afford to fall for? I mean look at us! Paul had holes all throughout his body, Ren was a cripple, and I still somewhat looked like I was lit on fire from those goddamn hives. What if this was the clue that we couldn't solve? But at the same time, nothing had happened yet. We had yet to run so fast that we got out of the cave or went to the next level. From what we could see, nothing dangerous was behind us, and if we didn't save our energy, we weren't gonna successfully fight anything off anytime soon.

"Fine," I exhaled before my feet stumbled to a halt. "Put Ren down. Let's both hold him."

"No, it's okay," said Ren, holding up his palm. "I can limp. It's not that bad. Save your strength."

"We gotta keep walking, guys. We could pass out if we don't." Shockingly, nobody argued. The energy between the three of us shook from our sweat and moans, while we internally screamed in pain from our lack of fuel.

"We need to find food," Ren mumbled.

"No," I snapped. "We need to find water." He was too smart to think that I was wrong.

"How long do you think we've been down here?"

My perception of time was, usually, on freaking point, but with the lack of varying visuals, plus the fact that I'd been with the same two people for probably two days now, my guess was probably way too warped. But a shrug satisfied him.

"Anyone fancy a game?" Paul randomly asked.

"Seriously?" I responded, refusing to admit that I secretly did have an interest. Depending on the game, of course.

"I always had a soft spot for twenty questions," Ren added.

"Didn't we all?"

"Right, then." Paul slapped his hands together, with a person, place, or thing in mind.

"Are you thinking of a person?" Ren asked.

"Yes."

"Halle Berry." One of the first things that Ren learned about Paul was his obsession with Halle Berry. I would be surprised if he could name five more actresses. Period.

"Bloody hell. Why do you always have to ruin the fun?"

"Attempt. This was an attempt to have fun. And like I said, I've always had a soft spot for this game. I'm good."

I mean, he wasn't wrong. Somehow Ren's severe allergy to fun repeatedly ruined the moment.

"What else can we play?" I asked.

"Well we -" But before Ren could finish, the smallest white noise I ever heard completely overloaded our senses. The ticking time bomb burst the second we whipped our eyes over the tense shoulders that still somehow stood above the rest of our bodies. Louder and louder the white noise grew. Way too fast if you ask me. What was one supposed to do when a swarm of bees raced towards you faster than your eyes could handle? No. Scratch that. A swarm of *giant* bees with deep gold and green eyes that reflected the tiger's almost perfectly. But the best part? The stripes on their backs weren't yellow like normal. They were the closest color to blood I'd ever seen.

"Oh, so that's what run means," Ren commented with a cracking voice, looking like he was about to faint.

"FUCKING SHUT UP! GOOO!" I screamed, or at least I think I did. Paul scooped up Ren once again, but I didn't even bother to ask permission to scoop up the other half of him. Goddamn, we must have looked like idiots. Ren certainly looked like he was being kidnapped in a cartoon. The natural droop in his face also didn't help.

They were getting closer, but we still maintained distance. Firebolts sprouted from their energy. Some sort of force both pulled and pushed them toward us. Someone was definitely starving them, just like the tiger.

"KEEP A LOOK OUT FOR AN OPENING!" Paul screamed over the increasing noise of hungry bees. Did bees even eat anything else besides pollen? Was it pollen?

"YEAH BECAUSE THOSE HAVE BEEN REALLY HELPFUL FOR US SO FAR!" I screamed back.

"WELL, I HIGHLY DOUBT WE'RE GONNA OUTRUN THE BLOODY SUCKERS!"

Something tickled my insides after hearing that word. *Outrun*. OUT - run. Hm. The clue didn't say outrun. Just run. Simple. Too simple. Run. Run where? Time to get creative.

"Paul! Follow me!" I said while I started turning around, probably too quickly. A heads up probably would have been the smarter choice.

"WHAT? ARE YOU CRAZY?"

"Paul! You can stop yelling now, I can hear you! Just follow me!" And he did. With a little more influence than I initially wanted to, but Paul needed a punch in the arm every once in a while.

"What's your plan now?" Paul asked, thinking I didn't have an answer. Idiot.

"Run into them!"

"What?!"

"Well, we're gonna duck obviously!" But Paul's blurry face suggested otherwise.

"Bloody hell," he mumbled. "No, we can't. We can't duck. That couldn't possibly be the closure to the puzzle. They want us to run into them! The clue wasn't to run and duck. It was just to run!" He was right. He had to be. The reassurance of our survival? Now that was still up in the air.

"Ren," I said to him quietly, even though he probably couldn't hear me since his face was unintentionally muffled into Paul's jacket. "I really hope you're not allergic to bees."

And with a whip of the head, my lifelong dream of never having to see a giant, bloodsucking bee up close came to an end. But the image almost moved in slow motion. Like we were underwater and had just heard at a young age that our favorite grandparent died. The live version of a nightmare popping out of your television.

I didn't know how well bees could see or not, but I refused to let them see the fear tucked away behind my eyes. They were getting the full *downward chin, forehead further ahead than the eyes* look. You know...superhero shit.

With arms pumping harder and more overly exaggerated than they did in junior high track, and fingertips shooting out from my palms, the three of us mentally counted down.

Three, two, - and instead of being stung by four possessed bees at a time, at least ten nearly knocked me to the ground.

"AHH!" I screamed, trying to get the bees out of my face while still running with occupied arms. Somehow, I found myself still standing, but still fluctuating with my balance. The swarm appeared endless. I could feel pinches and slaps, but a full-on sting had yet to impale me. Or at least that's what my brain would let me process. The pain probably wouldn't fully sink in until the overwhelming sensation of not being anywhere else disappeared.

"KEEP PUSHING!" Paul went back to screaming. Even if we survived we needed to keep moving our feet forward in order to get to the next step.

Bees' wings are a lot stronger than I thought they were. The bristle-like spikes sticking out of them kept scraping across my skin and splashed little spots of blood everywhere. It was the last thing that I wanted to admit, but the best thing to do was to keep repeating Paul's voice in my head. "KEEP GOING!" or whatever it was. I wasn't usually keen on listening to him when he spoke.

The pain was tolerable for now, but I lost faith in our ability to step one foot in front of the other. There was still a swarm of bees to push through. Though, the last thing that I needed was to look back and acknowledge our progress.

With the population of bees growing by the second, the area surrounding us was becoming suffocating. I had no desire to breathe in a bee the size of my head either. Maybe that wasn't possible, but with how everything was playing out in this place, I wouldn't have been surprised if these assholes figured out a way to do it. Plus, with all these wings flapping every which way, dirt from the ground and the walls shot straight into my eyes, almost blinding me.

"Almost there," Paul managed to cough up.

I almost asked him, "How the fuck do you know that?" But then I heard it. The puncturing and violent noise was dying down. Not by much. At least not yet anyway. Then came the decrease in population. I couldn't see them, but I could feel fewer wings and stingers whipping across my face and body. We were close, but my confidence in not passing out beforehand did not increase. Not by a single notch. If we were to stop at all, we could risk losing our chance to fulfill the riddle and we could be stuck here for longer or forever.

Breathe, just breathe, I thought. Oxygen was the only thing that could possibly help me at this point. The best guidance I would ever give my nursing patients. The funny thing was, I didn't say this out loud, but someone heard me. It wasn't Ren or Paul, though. They never listened to me in general, but it was as if someone was reading my mind and I could sense their presence in my head.

The ghost pushing buttons in my brain was trying to get me to do something, I just couldn't tell what it was. There was no voice, just some sort of spirit, lingering in my body just waiting to boss me around.

And then I felt it. There was nothing psychically there. At least it wasn't anything made of solid, liquid, or gas. Something way more advanced than that. A strong, and I mean *strong* force pushed me forward, like it was helping me. It knew I desperately needed that help too. Ren may have been connecting Paul and I together in a way, but Paul was only ever concerned with himself.

They weren't hands either. Just...an essence. An essence of care and encouragement. That was the only thing that helped me through those last few steps through the thick, deafening swarm of bees.

"Chess?" I vaguely heard Paul say. "Chess, you alright?" It wasn't until the last syllable of that sentence that my distraction faded.

"What? Yeah, I think so." Still catching my breath, I sensed maybe two or three more bees passing us, but since we basically had already passed the test, or whatever they wanted to call it, they might have already been instructed to leave and continue forward.

It wasn't until after we put Ren down that I realized how insanely sore my arms were. A hundred push-ups didn't even compare to this amount of constraint. I almost couldn't fully stretch them out.

"You're bleeding like a madwoman," Paul complained before he blotted his sleeve all over my face. I would have told him that he should look at his own face, but I didn't even like having pimple scars on my face let alone deep cuts from the wings of giant bees. You know, the usual stuff.

"Ren, you good?" I asked him, but before he could answer, we were once again cut off by the sudden shake of a platform lifting us up to the next step of the tunnel.

The crumbling sounds didn't grow louder the higher we went like they usually did. Something about my ears refused to let me stay conscious throughout the short journey. I was about to faint, I could tell. I wanted to slip in one more attempt to ask Ren if he was okay, but right before my knees released their firm stance, I turned around to see no one there to catch me.

"Ren? Paul?" I was alone, and before I could see where I currently was, my upper left arm collided with the rough floor and my vision blurred into black.

11:
PAUL

"Hello?" I called out before opening my eyes. "Hello?" I repeated when no one answered. *Of course. Why wouldn't this happen?*

I pulled myself up regardless of the soreness and proceeded down the tunnel. Of course, they probably went on without me just to see what was ahead, but the further I got, the more accustomed I was to being alone, which scared me half to death.

I seriously wanted something or someone to jump right out at me, just as long as it wasn't that bloody tiger again. Something or someone needed to give me a hint. That was the whole wretched point of us staying together, so we could all know the clue no matter who heard it. Nonetheless, I proceeded to walk. The only thing I could do. *Step, step, step...step.*

Thank God that light grew a spec bigger, though it almost hurt my eyes, believe it or not. Nothing meditative ever came from light. I was always the person that preferred dim light in both social and isolated settings. Maybe that was only from growing up in dreary old England, but it didn't assist in diminishing my fear. Something about walking towards a bright light didn't bring me any comfort, funnily enough.

Step, step, step.

No. I couldn't take the silence anymore. The silence made my shoulders and finger tips twinge so uncomfortably, I, for once, craved the sound of Ren talking about something daft, or rubbish. A terrible, terrible thing to wish for that I prayed never to wish for again.

Something needed to stimulate my senses. Something. Anything.

"*Hmmmmm,*" I hummed. Weak. I needed a threatening tune that established my dominance over every creature that probably wasn't coming for me. "Happy birthday to you..." There we go. Creepiest song I knew.

The hour went faster than I thought. I guesstimated the hour because I went through the first hour of *The Wolf of Wall*

Street in my head. Damn good movie. But something rudely interrupted my fantasy.

Wooooosh...

The white, meditative noise that I needed. Maybe an A.C.? That would have been lovely since I was sweating like a pig over here. But the closer I got, the more uneven the noise rippled. The intensity rocked back and forth like a boat on an...ocean. Bloody hell, it was a goddamn ocean. Maybe not a real or authentic ocean, but it was water. Big bowls of water, with the vibrant sound of an indoor pool.

Unfortunately, along with water, comes mosquitos and other nasty creatures. I was already bleeding enough. I didn't need more tiny holes in me.

"Ah, ya little bugger!" I said, repeatedly smacking my hands and face. Thank the lord I brought a jacket.

The salty smell overwhelmed my nose to the point that I almost had to shove my face into my shirt. I was getting close. Maybe I would have found some sort of clue once I was there, or even better, (better would probably be a stretch) Chess and Ren might be there. But the more I thought about it the more terrified I was at the possibility that somebody would show up, and it wouldn't be Chess or Ren.

My footsteps caused echoes that crescendoed louder and louder with every roll of the foot. I pictured the body of water to have one giant, slow, dramatic reveal, but due to the lack of light, I was centimeters away from falling in. The sound of small ripples were the only warning signs that I was getting too close.

"Whoa!" I hollered before I caught my balance. My guess was that the platform was one giant drop off instead of a ramp of sand leading me to the water. Like a pool, only with less safety regulations. Luckily if I did fall, it would only be a few inches to the water, but I managed to stay dry for the time being.

Slowly, my eyes adjusted to the room's minimal light. I couldn't see the light at the end of the tunnel anymore. If something was blocking it, the darkness covered it up. My only choice to escape or to find the crew was to keep walking along the edges of the platform that met the water. Bloody suckers probably thought I would have given up by now or accidentally fallen in.

"Chess? Ren?" I started calling out softly until I realized they wouldn't be able to recognize my large booming voice unless I gave it my all. "CHESS? REN?" Meh. Better.

If they did respond, I couldn't hear them. I couldn't help but think that maybe I was the only one who made it up to the next level free. What if they were captured, or knocked out? The possibility seemed more than just an option, it toyed with me even though it was an expected enigma. It was more than just feasible. The fear urged me to run instead of walk once again.

The ache in my feet grew quicker than before and more than I expected. Lord, I was falling apart. Regardless of how lucrative this industry was, I was getting too bloody old for it. I was surprised to admit that this was the first time I thought of retirement throughout this little adventure. Not sure how that was possible, but it was comforting to think about in the back of my head. Sunny days in paradise. Endless trips back to London. I was sure Chess hadn't stopped thinking about retirement this whole time. Lazy fuck.

A few minutes into the stroll along the water, I suddenly took notice of some splashing with my steps and of the hole in the sole of my shoe. It wasn't large, but water started getting into it, and the small draft was getting quite breezy.

"Ah, bugger." I crouched down to examine the tragedy when my stomach rumbled the moment I hunched over. My hunger spiked within a half a second.

Well then, I thought. *Let's see what this water has to offer.*

Like most humans, I like to cook my fish, but I would bloody well settle for food poisoning over this much starvation. And if there were any fish in there, I hoped there was enough for Chess and Ren too. Especially Ren, since he always whines when he's hungry.

I had never cared much for swimming with bare feet, so I left my shoes on and only took off my torn-up jacket that was barely keeping me warm.

One toe at a time, my body crept into the chilly water that, more than likely, wasn't going to be very kind to me. Now up to my shoulders, my feet still didn't touch the floor. How deep did this bugger go?

The painful, and somewhat bothersome thought crossed my mind that I was probably gonna need to swim deep under to find or see anything. Contrary to the popular belief among my mates, I was never the most talented swimmer. The thought of nothing but water surrounding me also put me in an uncomfortable position. What if I needed to...you know...breathe?

"Bloody hell," I mumbled before I took the deepest breath possible and submerged myself into the water. The water was surprisingly a normal temperature, but I gently shivered anyway. No discomfort yet, but the more I swam, the less hope I had of finding food. What was I to do? Feel them out? Grab them with my bare hands? But that was the only option at this point, wasn't it?

Gradually, my breaths became shorter and shorter while my heartbeat grew more audible. Every muscle in my body needed a break before the water pulled me down for good.

Keep going, keep pushing, I told myself as I headed back to the surface. *Only a few more feet.*

There was only a fraction of pain when my palms dramatically collided with the sharp edges of the tunnel floor. My lungs clawed in a painful breath. Though I could hardly acknowledge it during my coughing fit, trying to get all of the water out of my mouth, my tongue and taste buds noticed something odd (as if that were a thing anymore). The water tasted normal. Not normal as in ocean normal. Normal as in from the fountain normal. Careful not to puke my brains out, I licked the surface like a dog. Fresh water. Bastards.

The idiots thought they could trick me by shoving the smell of the Atlantic Ocean up my nose. Or maybe this was just part of their game. That had to be it. Otherwise they could have just made it real salt water. Anything in this hell was able to be manifested.

The only other time I'd been this desperate for water, and went overboard once I got ahold of it, was the first time I walked around Times Square in the dead of heat. I had forgotten my wallet, and when I went back to the hotel, I made myself sick with the liters of water my body devoured. I couldn't afford to make that same mistake.

Somehow pacing the large gulps of water shortened my breath even more. Damn. Licking water, panting. I really was such a dog, wasn't I?

The water was mesmerizing. If I examined it, I could see the reflection of my shiny, dreamy eyes. But something took those dreamy eyes of mine by surprise. A dreadful, suicidal surprise.

The more I squinted, the more I could see the tiny light at the bottom of the oversized pool's floor. The scarce light stayed small, yet still apparent. That was it. The bottom of this bloody ocean. That was my way out of this part of the tunnel. The bottom didn't seem too far down, but as Chess commonly said, I needed to be dramatic first.

Maybe I was wrong. Maybe I hadn't thought it through enough. A lovely endeavor really, until another surprise struck me more unpleasantly than a bolt of lightning. Much, much more unpleasantly.

"*Dive, dive DIVE, dive,*" the dainty voice echoed, unwelcome in my ear. There it was. The reassurance I was not asking for.

It sounded strange, but I needed to think of the worst possibilities. What could possibly happen that would torture me to my breaking point? Discomfort in the lungs?...Just calm down. Dizzy focus?...Just shake my head awake. It was the only way according to Siri over here.

"Come on, mate," I said to myself out loud. "Ready?" Nope. "Three, two, one."

12:
REN

Either Chess or Paul must have heard the clue by now, I thought. But where the hell were they? It had been hours and somehow it was getting cold. Really. Cold. And being from Florida, no matter how many layers I had on, I was never fully satisfied with my warmth.

The limping was somehow getting worse. You'd think being in an environment where you could see your breath, the air would feel like an ice pack to injuries, but no. It could never be that easy. Not with me. Hell, not with *us*!

What could this stupid clue possibly be? And was this another hallucination? Or dream?

After maybe two hours, I told myself more often that I needed to stop thinking so much and simply observe what was happening around me. Nothing overly animated moved along the tunnel, but I couldn't shake the feeling that someone else was here. Not that they were necessarily watching me, but it resembled the common feeling of simply being in a grocery store. Most likely no one was staring at you, but someone could also blindly run into you when turning the corner.

If Chess and Paul were running the same race that I was, they probably weren't stopping. If I wanted to keep up with them, I couldn't stop either. No matter how much pain I was in.

I went through the list of outcome possibilities. One: when we reunite, someone would need saving, and due to statistics, it would probably be me. Two: we would all be able to see each other, but would be separated and not be able to touch or help each other. (That's usually the most popular scenario in cinematic experiences.) Or three: basically, number two, but instead of being separated from each other, we all would fall into a ditch before we could reach each other. Only this ditch would lead us back to the beginning, and we would have to start all over again...or something of the sort.

Chess was probably thankful that she was alone right now, unless Chess and Paul had managed to stay together. Although, I highly doubted it. That wouldn't be the same strategic manipulation that I was used to, but Chess always wanted to do things alone. Her control issues drove her to prefer it that way.

When we first met, she tried to manipulate this cop into letting her pass an excluded area in a concert, so she could act as a hair stylist and steal a singer's necklace. Not our typical "con" job, but John knew some people working the concert and made it clear to us that they were easy to manipulate and, I quote, "dumber than most of the actors in Hollywood on meth," whatever that meant. I was too uncomfortable to ask.

Anyway, we had a plan to go in all together to make ourselves look more important, and at the last minute, Chess changed her mind and said, "Wait here." We didn't argue since it was a last-minute job on our day off, but when she came running back with the necklace and the same cop chasing her, we instantly regretted not going with her. But in any case, we got away, and that necklace wrote us all beautiful paychecks that we blew on a trip to Greece. Aaaand of course, our cons continued there. Let's just say that Greek people are too damn nice.

Ever since then, I diligently, and regularly put in effort to make Chess trust me more. She trusted Paul, but always got the impression he was trying to upstage her. I never upstaged her. Not even close, but she still never fully trusted me. We probably could have made much more money if none of these issues had existed. Although, on the other hand, maybe our tense relationships with each other was what had got us this far. The need and urge for validity kept us sharp and pushed us to take the next step forward. Literally, in this case.

Somehow thinking about this story distracted me from my pain, and I took into account how little I'd been wobbling like a marionette. The pain wasn't at ease quite yet, but I was able to tolerate it and ignore it more.

Alright, I thought. *What's another stupid story about Chess that I can make fun of her for later? More distractions, more distractions, more distractions.*

And with the next breath I took, I certainly got quite the distraction.

"Oh no," I mumbled through gritted teeth. It was the gut-wrenching smell of the ocean. Let me clarify this. I hate the ocean. All of them. The Pacific, Atlantic, even the Ocean movies with George Clooney and Sandra Bullock. Every. Last. One.

When I was a teenager, I even wrote down a list of reasons as to why. No particular order, but here's how it went; the smell, the immensity, the smell, my allergies to fish and coral, the smell, sharks, and last but not least, the smell.

I'd say it was just the smell that made me sick to my stomach, but no. Everything on that list made me nauseated in one way or another. Some from fear, others from that goddamn, freaking smell!

I couldn't hear the sound of water yet, but I knew it was coming soon. But why? Did we finally walk so far, we reached the coast? Actually, that wouldn't be entirely incredible, but the majority of this tunnel was an illusion. I'd be surprised if it was even 10% geologically accurate.

The air was now moist, and somewhat more breathable. Just as long as I didn't breathe through my nose, of course. The light at the end of the tunnel was no longer visible, but a different light was. The rippling water almost gave off a sort of glare. Similar to a midnight ride out on a boat at sea. The closer I got to the surface, the closer I was to realizing the light must have been coming from under the water. And, of course, that could only mean one thing; *That's where the journey is to be continued.*

Just like Paul crawling over that invisible glass wall. Only this time, we were to go under something. Or maybe the tunnel continued to a new surface. A surface where Chess and Paul or for the love of God, *anyone* could have been. These people knew I couldn't swim. At least not well. Torture. That's what they were trying to do to me, torture! That and utter humiliation, but in case you couldn't tell, I would take humiliation over torture any day. I wasn't used to torture. Well...not as much.

The time has come, I thought. *The time has come for me to finally embrace what Paul would do in this situation.* By far the last person I wanted to channel, but what other choice did I have? That man pushed past his fears every single time, except for when it came to needles. He still hadn't fully admitted that, but otherwise, I think I would have seen his anchor tattoo that he's been talking about getting for the past five years.

On top of his ability to shake his fears, he's also quite optimistic. Rather the exact opposite of Chess in most situations.

What would he do? What would he say to himself? After asking myself those two questions over and over again, I had an idea. A single idea that was mediocre at best, but it was something. Okay, you've been running a lot. *Your VO2max is amazing right now. You can hold your breath for as long as you want.* This wasn't going to solve most of my problems, but it was a start.

Time was running out. What if the others were waiting for me on the other side of whatever it was and running out of oxygen? Keeping up with them was crucial.

Wait, running out of time? That was it. I needed to simply save time. That would help my lungs, decrease my allergic reactions, and save my poor muscles that barely existed. I needed to *dive.* Now if only I knew *how* to dive. That might come of use.

As quickly as my limp foot could carry me, I backed up to the wall for a running leverage. I couldn't remember the last time I worked out, but knowing my arms were about to do most of the work, I started bending them every which way to warm up, hoping I wouldn't hurt those too. That would have been some useful knowledge to get out of Paul as well.

Suddenly, my chest stiffened to the point that I physically had to tell myself to breathe, or else, I would, for sure, drop dead.

With a few thumps on the deflated chest, an impersonation of a bull, and a few scuffs of the good foot, I gathered up just enough confidence to push off into my sprint.

Big breath before the dive, that's all I had to focus on at this point. The water grew brighter, the waves increased in volume, and about ten feet before the break of the surface, I took the most cartoon-like, audible breath in through my mouth, and completely forgot to dive. But nonetheless, driving yourself into water feet first will surprisingly get you far.

It was too late to think about it. I had enough oxygen, or I hoped I did. Wherever the light was coming from, the light's brilliance almost made me believe the first layers of my eyeballs were about to fall off. But the light was performing the two most important jobs of all: One, reassuring me that there were no sharks or even fish in this body of water. Two, that reassurance pulled my focus so far away, I almost didn't realize how far I had made it under water.

13:
CHESS

It was obvious. Jump in the water and down through the hole. It probably took those idiots a second to figure that out. God, I hoped it was Paul that got the clue. The clue was probably "swim" or something stupid like that. Curious though. Why was it so easy? Or at least I thought it was. It was the only way forward. Or maybe...what if the boys got a different test? But if that was so, why didn't I get a clue by now? We would have all gotten a different clue, right?

What if this was the end? This could be the trap these assholes were waiting for. The big finale that would certainly take us all down.

Damn it, Chessy. (I was the only one who could call me that.) *You're overthinking everything like Ren, and he's not even here.*

Before falling to my potential death, I paced back and forth within about a ten-foot range. Usually the only way I could think. The water didn't look too bad, and the small spot of light dropped the level of scariness by about fifteen percent.

Lucky for me, I liked sharks. Dolphins too of course, but after that tiger incident I highly doubted this was a dolphin-friendly place. Now the only question was: dive or cannon ball?...Definitely cannon ball.

Uncertain of how long I was about to separate myself from oxygen, I took the deepest breath I could, thinking of Adele when she told people to breathe with the stomach area, and made probably an almost decently sized splash. That was always the goal when doing a cannonball, right? God, why am I a child?

Ever since I was a kid, I always had this habit of swimming like a mermaid. The only thing that made having a pool worth it really. This time, the second my head plunged into the water, I was swimming more like a serial killer escaping from prison on an isolated island.

The immediate discomfort in the pressure hit me like a balloon popping in my face. The exposed skin on my ankles tingled to the point of numbness from how fast my feet kicked back and forth. And then there were my eyes. Oh crap, no. Not my eyes. I actually needed those to get out of here. But no matter how many times I blinked or how hard I rubbed them, the irritation kept me from keeping them fully open. The light growing brighter with every kick didn't help either. Not quite like staring into the sun, but I preferred the tiny little light that made us live like bats in the tunnel before.

Maybe this is it, I thought. The light was bigger than it ever was, and the overwhelming expansion continued like flying into the nightlights of Las Vegas.

Probably thirty seconds had passed. Finally, my lungs started to hurt, but that was a good sign. This was tolerable. For now. The rest of my body, minus my eyes of course, were still moving strong. But it would only stay that way if I stopped thinking about it.

Relax, I told myself. *Don't think, just zone out. Like you're a zombie flying in the wind.* Not sure why that was my analogy, but it worked. Or at least it did for the next minute or so.

The pain in my chest was too prominent to ignore now, but I was so close. Just a few more kicks and I'd be -

But just like turning off a giant television in the living room, the big light shut off. Just like that. Where in the hell could there be an off switch to that thing?

My feet stopped kicking in shock, and obviously a little bit of confusion. Thankfully, it made my lungs hurt a little less, but only a bit. I almost passed out from the sudden lack of movement. But something forced my eyes to refocus. Right at the exact same time, I abruptly saw both Paul and Ren swimming towards me, barely lit. Both of them looked way too happy in a way. Sort of a mixture between eager to rescue me and happy to see me for some reason, but no matter how dizzy I was, I wouldn't give them the satisfaction.

Hoping that they weren't an illusion or a trick, I got my feet back to kicking and stretched my fingertips towards them. Somehow, it didn't feel long at all as they both did the same for each other and me. A stupid looking triangle. That's what we were, but the highest level of stupidity was the level that reminded us we had no plan once we came back together.

The looks on our faces. Wow, morons. But I could see Paul was trying to tell us something. Well...he was trying to tell *me* something.

"Dive," he mouthed. "DIVE!" That must have been the clue that was whispered into Paul's ear. Suddenly flashbacks from literally a few hours ago burst in front of my face.

It's not what we think, said the voice inside my head. *It's a step further, the step that none of you want to take.* The bitch that's been putting clues into our ears didn't mean dive into the water, she meant dive once we were *in* the water. We had to dive even further down, and my lungs were on fire. I wasn't waiting for them. I beckoned the two to follow me, making the most exaggerated movement I possibly could have, and thank God, the two idiots understood what I was trying to tell them.

My ears began to hurt even more the deeper I went. I'd never been so desperate for anything. If we were wrong, we were dead. I saw no light whatsoever. It was a possibility I couldn't bear to think about.

Ren drifted a little far behind, but not enough for me to care or do anything about it. By now, it probably had been at least three minutes without air. I prayed that the boys felt stronger than I did at this point. If anything happened to me, maybe, just maybe they would have enough strength to at least guide me.

My legs weren't at full speed like they were before, but at least my feet pulled through for me. Something was coming. I could feel it. I didn't know what, but it was something.

I could almost feel my brain moving about my skull, I was so out of it, but all of a sudden, someone grabbed my arm. Who? I wasn't sure. Maybe Ren, maybe Paul, maybe somebody else, but they were scared. Something did happen, but I could barely feel it. All I noticed was that it felt like doing a somersault in the pool, but I wasn't doing it voluntarily. Someone was doing it for me, and it lasted way too long with water shooting up my nose.

My vision swirled in circles. Maybe my body was still flipping around, maybe it wasn't, but it was definitely pulling toward something. I didn't have to think about where I was going for long, because with the faint light, and lack of pressure in my ears, and the painful gasp for breath, I realized my surroundings flipped upside down, and I'd been pulled toward the surface.

"Ren? Chess?" Paul checked on us after he almost caught his breath.

Quickly, I saw Ren struggling to keep his head above the water, but he was there. Hopefully all of him too. "We're here. We're both fine." I usually hated it when he thought it was his job to check on us. Obviously, I had the whole thing under control.

"Where's the shore?" Ren asked.

I looked around while my eyes still adjusted, but Ren probably hadn't done that yet since there was a surface surrounding us in a perfect circle.

"Come on," I managed to say. "Let's just swim this way. We can do it." Sometimes I hated sounding like a fitness instructor, but it worked.

With the little strength we had left, we pulled ourselves up onto the rocky platform. I would have taken holding my body in a plank for five minutes with Paul sitting on my back over that shit.

The shakiness in my arms caused me to slip and hit my head on the hard, rocky platform. I was still so wet I couldn't tell if I was bleeding or not until I saw the gush of blood profusely drip onto the rocks.

"God damn it," I muttered, trying to pull my sleeve up enough to blot the wound. Not that it really helped. We were all beat-up disasters by now.

"Is everyone okay?" Paul asked, still fighting to pull himself out of the water.

"I'm fine," I lied way too aggressively. We waited for Ren to answer, but nothing. Only the sounds of the rushing water filled the room. "Ren?" I called out struggling to turn my aching body around to find him. "Ren?"

I'm not sure what the fuck Paul was doing, but out of the corner of my right eye I could see Ren flopped over the edge with his belly on the rocks and his feet dangling in the water. "You've got to be kidding me," I yelled out, scrambling over to him, once again feeling the burning in my lungs.

Paul finally caught on as to what was happening and dragged himself over, thinking he was gonna be helpful. Sometimes he thought his mansplaining overshadowed my nursing experience.

Ren was a lot heavier to flip over and manage with an overly dizzy head, but his almost blue lips told me he wasn't breathing. Damn it, Ren.

"Sorry, dude. This might hurt in the morning." My body was going to kill me for this, but Ren's best chance was for me to intertwine my fingers together, pull them up above my head like I was about to dramatically kill him with a sword, and plunge my fists so deep into his abdomen, the water had to come out. And of course, it did. Something I was surprisingly not allowed to do in nursing school.

"Geez," I think Paul said. I was more focused on Ren's frantic and continuous coughing. Thankfully, the color immediately returned to his lips.

"You okay?" I asked, aggressively patting his back, trying to get all of the water out.

"No," he coughed out. "You know I don't like people touching my stomach."

"You know what? I'm gonna take that as a thank you, because you're welcome."

The least comfortable surface in the world pulled me back down after I knew Ren was okay. There could have been a hurricane passing by for all I knew. I needed to sleep more, and I doubted I was the only one.

"We need to get to the next level already," I told them. "I need five days of sleep."

"Hate to break it to you, Chess," said Ren. "I think we are at the next level."

"Hate to break it to me? Fuck I'll just go to sleep now."

"Wait," Paul interrupted. "Let's get to a more secure area first. We don't know where this water is going.

"Fine," I agreed, reaching my hand out so he'd help me up.

"Also, one more thing." His wheels turned like he was trying to do simple division, but this was hopefully a more complex idea. "I have a theory. I think whoever deciphers the clue is the one who hears the next one."

Why didn't we figure this out before? I'll tell you why, we've been hungry and thirsty for days now and my legs were about to fall off soon. I don't pay attention to anything when a hamburger is not a short car ride away.

"Makes sense," I said. "I'll keep my eye out - or, you know what I mean. Now let's get out of here, so I can sleep."

"Right, but that's the thing," Paul continued. "I don't think you should sleep just in case you miss it."

"Are you serious?" Unfortunately, he was. He would often think that he could tell me what to do. "I need to sleep."

"We can't risk losing the next clue."

"Ren heard a clue when he was asleep!"

"Yeah, by luck! What if he hadn't?" I didn't answer. He had a point, but why would I give him the satisfaction? "Wait," Paul interrupted. Again. "One more thing. The water is fresh drinking water." Okay, he was forgiven.

14:
REN

Due to Chess's loud pacing and soccer games with pebbles, I couldn't sleep. And yes, I did ask her to please stop, but the response she gave was simply, "No." That was all. No explanation. I was almost tempted to whisper a clue into her ear with a slightly higher voice than mine, but my face would receive the gift of a decent-sized dent in it if I had.

"Anything yet?" Paul asked for the fourth time.

"Ask me that one more time. I fucking dare you," Chess responded in one of her common tones. Paul looked too tired to respond. He could usually sleep heavier than a rock, but his anxiety was probably what kept him up. Though he would never admit it.

Seeing the bags puff from her eyes made the guilt significantly worse. She made it quite clear that if she were to lie down, she would instantly fall asleep, and she wasn't in the mood to be woken by me, and especially not Paul.

"What's taking so long?" Chess complained. "It's been hours." I opened my mouth, about to answer until Chess cut me off. "Don't answer that. I just need to complain for a while."

"Chess," Paul finally spoke. "Why don't you just lie down, and we'll talk to you to keep you awake?" Initially, she didn't like that idea, and she made that physically apparent with every muscle in her body, but even Chess was able to compromise on occasion.

"Fine, but I pick the topics."

"Wouldn't have it any other way." With Paul's blaring volume and his thick accent, his sarcasm was usually difficult to read.

"Talk to me about your favorite book."

I assumed Paul didn't read, and due to my lack of knowledge about the man, I began to consider what I've read recently until he spontaneously responded, shocking us both.

"I personally love the last Harry Potter book."

"The last one?" Chess asked with her chin dropped and eyes scrunched.

"Yeah, what's wrong with that?"

"It's just...depressing!"

"Yes, but a brilliant depressing."

"He has a point," I added, unaware that that was apparently the wrong addition to the discussion, and only realizing this after Chess circled her disgusted look all the way over to me. But it was true after all.

After a few more pointless altercations that I didn't pay attention to, I noticed a bit of pressure shooting from my bad ankle into my calf. My irrational senses drove me to believe it was going to pop in one way or another. Chess was the last person that I wanted to annoy right now, or at any time truthfully, but what more could I possibly do to her?

"Hey, Chess," I said, already screaming with my body language that I was suddenly in a lot of pain.

"Whaaaat?" She wailed in overdramatic agony. I suppose I was wrong about the whole, what-more-could-I-do-to-her thing.

"Something feels wrong. I don't know what, but I think it's swelling, and it's kind of going numb.

"Hold on, let me look. It's probably just the temperature change. I don't think it's anything to worry about." In the time it took for me to take two long deep breaths in, Chess had already concluded everything was fine, and her guess was completely valid.

It wasn't necessarily the speed that caught me off guard in a way; it was the natural state of caring she suddenly slid into. But it was always like that whenever she had to look at something abnormal or an injury on someone. She became a completely different person in my eyes, or in anyone's eyes really.

"Hey, I got a question," I stated, expecting her to immediately respond with a sharp "no" just like before.

"What?" Oh, wow. I hadn't prepared the phrasing of the question yet. Here went nothing.

"Why did you quit being a nurse?"

It was as if no one had ever asked her that before. No one cared. Or more likely, everyone was too scared to ask. The question didn't anger her. Not yet anyway, but it did upset her in a way that I'd never seen before. From the way she looked at me with such regret and despair, I probably wasn't ready for the answer.

With steadiness and slow pacing, her vocal chords managed to slip out, "Why do you ask?"

"Oh, come on. You're too good at this to be fired for being incompetent or anything." The drop in her eyebrows suggested I might have been on the right track. "Chess, I'm sorry. I didn't mean to piss you off. It's none of my business."

"No. It's fine. Might as well since we're slowly dying in this hell hole." She tried to get comfy snuggling upward against the wall as she began her story. "I tried to block most of this out, but I was twenty-three, and we just won a strike that every single one of the nurses protested in. We wanted better wages, and after only a week of striking, we won. It was pretty awesome, and I thought everything was gonna be all fine and dandy.

"A few weeks go by, and I have this new patient. His name was Earl, and I will never forget the look on his face whenever I came in. He was only my patient for a little while, but he constantly told me how much I reminded him of his daughter who was studying abroad at the time. Her name's Lilly. He always said her name with such love and admiration. Just two syllables, but I always wanted someone to say my name that way.

"Anyway, he had a heart condition. One day, I had to give him his usual dose of codeine. Fifty milligrams. I wasn't paying attention because I was listening to a story about Lilly, and I accidentally gave him morphine instead. It was meant for the patient next door to him. To make matters worse. I didn't even notice until his code blue alarm went off. He died so fast that there wasn't a speck of hope for him, and I didn't even get to say goodbye."

I was so afraid the silence was going to linger on for too long, and I would say the wrong thing to her, but luckily, Paul came to my rescue as usual.

"Did they ever find out it was you?" He asked.

"I'm not sure. Probably, but I moved everything out of my apartment literally that night and stayed with a friend for a while. I'm still surprised they haven't found me. I should be in jail for more reasons than one."

"I'm so sorry, Chess," I finally managed to blurt out. I'd never seen her look so numb.

"I couldn't get a real job after that, so I got a new bank account with my middle name as my first, and decided if I was gonna live with that on my shoulders, I might as well make a living knowing I don't deserve any of what I can get my hands on. And somehow if I were to get caught, it would sting a little bit less, knowing that I *did* deserve whatever came to me."

"Did you ever tell your friend?" Not to sound harsh, but I truthfully didn't know that Chess had any friends.

"No. She thought that I quit because I developed an allergy to latex." It wasn't an appropriate time to laugh, but we did anyway. Of course, Chess would make up a stupid excuse like that.

Chess had never looked sad in front of us before. I couldn't imagine feeling responsible for something like that for over, what? Five or six years now? We weren't pure, honest people. I don't think we ever were, but we never brought a gun to a job. We never planned on even knocking someone out to rob them. We *never* physically hurt anyone.

"Do you think someone in Earl's family could have created this tunnel to get revenge on you?" Paul blurted out. He must have thought Chess and I were thinking that too, but Chess made it clear that was anything but the truth.

"What?" She asked. "No. He was one of the few people that I allowed to call me Harriet. When I changed my name with illegitimate documents, I didn't leave any traces. And besides, I don't think Earl even knew my last name, let alone his daughter."

"That at least crosses one name off the list." Paul's continuous obsession with figuring out who was behind this was making my skin crawl. It was almost as if he cared more about the vengeance of his anger rather than his and our safety.

"Why don't we wait until we get out of here? Then we can worry about who did this," I suggested. Knowing Paul, I left my attitude behind as much as I could, but that didn't stop from having just a few drops drip from my mouth.

"I can't," he whispered. "It's like a tic now. Knowing I'm trying to figure it all out, that's what's getting me through. Otherwise, my anger will explode out of me. I swear it."

I couldn't object to that, but I didn't want to discuss it any further either.

"Fine," said Chess. "Talk about it all you want."

"Actually," Paul mumbled. "I guess I could temporarily distract myself with more pain and stress."

We'd already laughed a few times at subtle jokes. This was not one of those times.

"Since we're coming clean about some things. I guess I could tell you why I left England."

Chess and I read each other's minds right at that moment. We both were apparently too ethnocentric to realize there must have been a reason why he left instead of there being a reason why he came.

"Welp, that sounds like a good start," said Chess.

"Okay," he began. "I was actually married for a little while. Her name was Jane. I loved her with my whole heart, but she didn't feel the same way. She never did. It took me way too long to figure that out. Pathetic really. She was a vet. She loved animals. One of my favorite things about her. She cared for so many living beings, not just people. So, when she left, I didn't understand why she couldn't care about me the same way.

"Anyway, before she left, I told her we should travel all around the United Kingdom, and then maybe, just maybe, move to America. She kept lying and told me that was her dream. It wasn't. I don't know what it was, but that wasn't it. Eventually she met someone else and moved out in the snap of a finger, just like that. She didn't even seem to care at all. I walked around London all day that day, not knowing where to go, or what I was doing. The funny thing is, the next time I tried walking around London again, I couldn't. All I remembered was pain. So, I got on the next plane to wherever in America, and I didn't look back. I just wanted to do something without her to prove to her and myself that I could be without her too and be happy. I didn't want her to steal that away from me."

The silence lingered for a few seconds. Paul clearly understood his tragedy didn't compare to accidentally killing someone. His failure to keep eye contact made that clear, but something happened after he finally took a deep breath. He looked *relieved*. Maybe it was because he finally got it off his chest, or maybe he took a moment to realize how far he had come without Jane.

"I'm really happy you decided to come to Atlanta," I said. "We wouldn't have made as much money if we didn't have you." The three of us finally exchanged genuine laughter. Nothing extraordinary, but it was a start after revealing such intense stories. Before I could change the subject, Chess chimed in.

"Hey, I've actually got a good idea," said Chess, chiming back in from her depressed reality, and trying to change the subject to a happier note. "What does everyone wanna do once we're the fuck outta here? And don't say 'eat a burger' or shit like that. What do you wanna *do*?"

Alright, this was without a doubt something I was okay with discussing. Some hopeful and exciting banter would do us well, but I couldn't think of a single thing. Once again, Paul came to my rescue with some ideas.

"I wanna take a trip," he said. "Maybe just rent a van or something and drive around the country. Get as far away from here as possible. At least for a little while."

Chess didn't even hesitate a second for her chance to propose her plans. "I'm going to Vegas." That was it.

"Chess, you've been to Vegas a hundred times."

"And all I've wanted to do for the past three or so days is go back for my hundredth and first time."

Paul's frustration with Chess's lack of creativity ended with him slouching over his straightened legs as if her decisions had any effect on him.

"What about you, Ren?" He asked, dramatically lifting his focus towards me. "What are you going to do?" An idea popped into my head, but it probably wasn't going to ring true when the time came.

"I'm going to smoke as much weed as I possibly can until...well until I don't feel like it anymore."

The dead silence they gave me made me believe they were too shocked that I would even say such a thing that they needed a minute, but that wasn't quite it.

"No, you won't," Chess shook her head like a disappointed mother.

"Yeah, alright," I agreed. "I'll probably just relax more and watch a few movies that I've been meaning to watch."

"Sounds about right, but for now, no resting for you. I need just a five-minute nap while you keep watch."

15:
CHESS

A part of me wished I never told them anything about why I quit being a nurse. They were the first people I ever told, but it kinda made sense in a way. They were the only few people I'd had in my life since it all went to shit. But I still had yet to decipher my feelings about "letting it all out," as the therapists say.

Luckily, they knew me well enough by now that I preferred people not saying anything at all than the wrong thing, but that didn't mean the wrong thing wasn't coming eventually. Ren did sometimes get a little too nosy.

"Anybody need to rest?" I asked before Paul could.

"Maybe in a little bit," Ren replied. "Just to stretch." I'm tempted to tell him stretching probably wasn't the best thing for his ankle, but, for real, I refused to gather up the energy to do so.

"I think it's almost been three days," Paul mumbled, and for a moment, I swear I could almost see him limp, but only for dramatic purposes. "Three days with no food."

"But we had water," I reminded him. "Water is more important than food, but that's why we have to rest more often."

"We should have eaten that tiger," Ren added, probably not thinking that sentence through first.

"Yeah? With what oven?"

"My loins," Paul answered. The three of us suddenly stopped, and with flawless comedic timing, we all joined in on synchronized laughter. Damn. Paul's jokes usually weren't that funny.

"Anybody able to turn on their phone yet?" Paul asked, looking for his own. Scrambling through his jacket pockets.

"I checked a few minutes ago, but it probably got destroyed by the water anyway," I responded.

"You think this was ever a real job?" Ren chimed in.

"That's a stupid question, Ren."

"Well, then why else would we be given all these tests and riddles? For fun? For revenge?"

Three questions in a row. Sometimes Ren reminded me of my mother. Always questioning everything, being nosy in everybody else's business. And most importantly, no matter how many times I screamed, "I don't fucking know!" She never took a hint.

"What if it wasn't meant for us?" Paul suggested before I had time to snap at Ren. "What if it was somebody else who set the trap for the old man and his wife?" It wasn't a horrible suggestion. Sounded plausible, but wouldn't somebody have noticed by now? If that had been true, one of two things would have happened by now; either we would have been released, or we would be dead.

"John couldn't be the only one involved in this," Paul commented.

"We don't even know if this was John to begin with."

"I realize that, but listen. Who else has something against us, or needs something from us?

I hadn't thought about that before. *Needs something from us.* What someone could gain from trapping three people in a haunted house for days was beyond me, but we couldn't rule it out.

"If someone needed something they could have just politely asked," I told them.

"They could ask Paul or me," said Ren, defensively. "But you? No. Absolutely not. You would have walked so fast past them, you probably would have knocked them over solely with your attitude."

Not wrong, but before I could come up with some nasty comeback, I had a surprising and unwelcome voice in my ear instead.

"*Riiiiiip, rip, RIIIIIIIIP, rip,*" she echoed.

"Damn it," I whispered. "I don't like that." I immediately turned to the boys to tell them what I heard.

"Rip?" Paul asked. "Are you sure? That sounds a lot more violent than the rest of them."

"Geez," said Ren. "What's around here that could rip?"

"Our clothes," Paul listed. "Or your penis," he continued saying to Ren. God, I could not wait to avoid men for five years minimum.

"Why not *your* penis?"

"Shut the fuck up, you goddamn perverts!" Although I could see Ren's point. "You know something's gonna randomly show up that we can -

But before I could finish, something caught my attention. Not so much a distraction, it just caught my eye and refused to let me go. With the metaphorical string that held attached from this object to my mouth and eyes, I lost complete control over them. No talking. Not even a single blink.

"Chess?" I heard Ren say. "What -" Then he saw it too. I couldn't do anything about it, but in my peripheral vision, he also turned his head to see in the close distance a clump of beautiful cloud-like materials falling onto the floor one by one. Like a magic carpet that you could float on. So mesmerizing. Even if I did have a choice, I don't think I would have wanted to blink or draw my attention away.

Three footsteps moved together in a daze closer and closer to these white blankets. That could only mean one thing; Paul was under the spell now too. All drunk on hypnotism together. No matter what we did, our loud feet crunched the sand beneath us at an even and steady pace, not slowing down anytime soon.

I couldn't have been the only one who's eyes were playing tricks on them. Unless, of course, there were multiple projectors stuck under the rocks and making the sheets of clouds turn the colors of Starburst candy.

Whoever was mind controlling us wasn't doing a very good job. I could still try and resist not walking over to the magic carpet looking clouds, but whatever I said or did, I had no say in the matter. Conscious, but the remote control was nowhere to be found.

One by one, the clouds floated to the ground faster and faster. That only made our feet pick up the pace. Or maybe they were coming closer to us. I couldn't focus enough to tell.

"Does anybody else - " I said involuntarily, and like a sleeping *My Little Pony*. " - want ice cream all of a sudden?"

"Yeah," I heard Ren respond. "Ice cream with a nap."

The fuck were we saying? And what were these things? I mean, I'm not completely stupid. I knew it was some sort of trap, but what kind of trap leads you to a cartoon fairy land filled with cotton candy? The only thing I could do was to just go along with it. If we didn't, there would be no clue. No clue, no level up.

"Mates," said Paul. "I think we should call it a day and snuggle up together." Dear Lord.

"I hope we can jump on them," I found myself saying. That was actually something I would have said without the mind control. *Blankets, comfort.* It all sounded so magical. Something I've been craving for three days.

Something tingled in my right index finger. Not a bad tingle. More of a resemblance to a dog sniffing you with their gentle, moist nose. But when I looked down in what felt like slow motion, I saw the multi-colored sparkles creep up along my skin and underneath my clothes.

"HAHAHAH," I uncontrollably laughed for a solid minute. What can I say? It tickled like hell.

"Let's never leave!" Ren splattered out with a clown-like grin spread across his face. Paul and I laughed in agreement while we waited for cloud blankets to fall right onto us. Why? I was exuberant to find out.

Glitter filled my nose as I saw a silhouette of a star shaped cloud slowly fall straight over my head. Giggle after giggle, I couldn't wait for the soft touch of the thick, fluffy substance. But inches away from my face, the cloud altered. Not physically, but its intentions cleared up straight away when the blanket pulled me to the ground and started to suffocate me.

Everything went dark. No more happiness. No more glitter. Just paralyzing and claustrophobic darkness. I could hear the boys being smothered to the ground with every drop of oxygen being vacuumed out of them.

This is it, I thought. *This is the final step. How we all go.* I could barely muster any noise while gasping for at least a little bit of air. But nothing. In a minute, we were all about to either be unconscious or dead.

What can I do? What can I do? My limbs eased back into my own control. Although they waved so frantically it was questionable.

"OW!" I screeched. My still tingly right hand hit something above my head. Someone's shoe. I could feel the leather. Paul's shoe. Welp, sorry, Paul. I had to do something, and my shoes were not in reach.

With just one hand I yanked the shoelace loose and began to pull. Those assisted pull ups at the gym were about to pay off.

Paul must have been confused and trying to say something since I could hear his muffled screams raise in pitch and his foot wouldn't stop kicking back and forth, but somehow that actually helped.

His boot slipped off so fast you would think it would rip through the cloud straight away. Nope. And no matter how much I banged against the blanket hoping it would pull away from my airways, nothing happened. Not even a pop. Not even a ripple.

I wanted to scream. If I was about to go, I was gonna evaporate with power. An effective virtue that wouldn't disappoint anyone. Especially the people trying to kill me. But I needed to preserve air. My hope wasn't gonna run out yet.

I tried to listen and be as still as I could. No point in struggling, so I might as well listen to see if I could hear Ren. Oh God, Ren. He was probably so scared like the little baby he was. Not the strongest either. If anybody was about to rip through these sheet clouds, I would have bet Betty White over him.

Once again, my lungs burned to no end. There were only a few more seconds to go. I didn't get a chance to take a deep breath like before in the water. The tests were getting harder. Honestly, I would have taken the tiger over this any day.

Meditate, I told myself. Somehow, somewhere, someone was telling me this was the only way to survive, or go out peacefully, but I was leaning more towards surviving.

The tingling in my fingers stopped. Instead, they slipped into a numbness that tricked me into thinking they weren't there. Now, I knew this couldn't be true, but I was wiping away from existence. Sinking into the earth where I'd be alone and still forever, but then I heard it. Somebody was here, or maybe somebody was free.

"*Reeeeeeeeep,*" I heard.

They were doing it! The clouds *were* able to rip, but with what? I didn't know, and I wasn't going to. They weren't going to get to me in time. Neither of these idiots knew C.P.R. I was about to die.

The light eased into a sort of watercolor image where everything blended together. Personally, I thought it was somewhat beautiful. I couldn't feel the burn anymore. Each little bit of my spirit trickled away, easing me into a peaceful numbness. Easy way to die, right? I thought so too until I gained consciousness again with Paul giving me mouth to mouth C.P.R. Welp, I stood corrected.

I wanted to yell at him to get off me, but I didn't have full control over my mouth let alone my vocal chords.

"Chess!" I heard Ren yell. "Chess, you're okay." Was I? I could cough, which meant I could breathe on my own again, but how many more times was I gonna come close to dying?

"Guys," I said after taking a few deep breaths. "I know it may not look like it, but I don't wanna rest. I wanna keep going. We need to get the fuck outta here."

16:
PAUL

I meant what I said about the ongoing compulsion of solving this one-of-a-kind mystery. Who could possibly create a tunnel underground that was probably thousands of kilometers long and could materialize anything from the real world or even from the back of their twisted minds to torture us along the way? But most importantly, why us? Or perhaps it was just a single one of us.

Even after that horrific story Chess told before, she still had to have plenty of secrets. Secrets she could be even more ashamed of.

And let's not forget about, "I'm secretly a smooth talker under all these computers" Ren. I never heard the story about how he joined the team. At first, for a while, it was just Chess and him performing small cons and stealing a few things here and there. Then one day, Chess walked me through the door and said, "This is Paul, he's contributing to our team now." After I exchanged some sort of awkward greeting with Ren, that was it. No questions. None. Ren didn't give a single damn.

However, Ren always seemed trustworthy. Whenever we needed something, he would do it in a heartbeat. After a few more clarifying instructions, of course, but he would do it. One time, when we were in Louisiana on a job, I was selling fake tickets to a basketball game. (I don't remember the name of the teams because I'm honestly not sure which American ball sport basketball was, but I was bollocks at hiding that lack of knowledge.) I needed Ren to get me basketball hats that we could sell along with tickets just in case someone else was there also trying to sell tickets, we would be offering a bundled deal.

Like I said, these tickets were fake, but they were damn good seats, so damn good money. Ren took this as a serious job that required going above and beyond. Instead of bringing me back two hats for two tickets, he brought me five packs of ten just in case people were interested in buying just the hats and so the three of us could keep one for ourselves. Unnecessary, but smart and thoughtful. As rubbish as it sounds.

Then there was Chess. Now don't laugh, but something about Chess reminded me of Hannibal Lecter from *Silence of the*

Lambs. Not that she would ever eat anyone, but from my perspective, she would perceive betrayal as below her. Truth and honesty, in the right situation, were important to her.

Even if it was just one of them, they would never admit it if somebody was after them. Hell, I probably wouldn't have admitted it either. Maybe that just goes to show you how well I did know these people after all. Hopefully, I had it all wrong.

"I'm parched again," I blurted out loud. No recent whispers passed our ears in hours. No. Maybe even a day. Probably time for a nap as well.

"Me too," Chess responded. "Hey. I gotta question." Both Ren and I patiently waited for her to ask her question, but we had to give a little, *Uh huh*, in order for her to continue. "Has anyone tried just -" And without giving a warning or completing her sentence, her long brown hair rippled back as the rest of her body burst forward and ran straight into the wall of the cave, right leg first.

"DAMN IT!" Chess screamed, realizing her one-hundred-twenty-pound body couldn't break through Saran Wrap, let alone a wall made of stone. "DAMN IT, DAMN IT, DAMN IT!" She finally lost it, but of course, it was only seconds before Ren and I joined in on going bonkers as well.

"LET US OUUUUUUUUT!" I screeched. And bloody hell it felt damn good.

Ren shouted so vigorously with his dry mouth I couldn't understand a word he was saying, but it almost sounded something along the lines of, "MY ASSHOLE HURTS, AND I MISS MY DOG!" Although I was quite certain he didn't have a dog.

Nothing came of our outbursts. Only bruised fists, sand falling into our eyes, and even more sore throats.

"Where do you think we are by now?" I asked them.

"If we went North?" Ren responded. "Canada. And if we went South, Antarctica. Maybe there will be some penguins we can eat."

"And if we went East or West?" Chess asked after a vicious cough attack.

"Actually, maybe we went full circle, and now we're just back in Atlanta."

None of us had the energy to laugh. We would still keep trying, but self-deprecating jokes about our pain and failures at this point weren't that amusing anymore. Not to sound like a five-year-old at camp, but we were terribly homesick.

"Paul," Chess called out to me. "I should take a look at your back. See if it needs new bandages."

"New bandages?" I asked, confused. "What would you use for new bandages? Everything on our bodies is filled with filth."

"Stop being so pessimistic!" She raised her voice. "I'll use my bra if I have to."

Unwilling to argue any further, I obeyed, lying face down on the ground. Oh, how I craved my bed. My memory foam, orthopedic, way too expensive bed. Screw all this traveling and bucket list crap. I would be ordering take out for the next three weeks without leaving my little nest.

"Ah!" I snapped after Chess poked her finger in one of my wounds. Not on, in. Infection galore. "Is it still open?"

"It's not as bad as it was, but you're gonna need stitches when we get out of here."

I waited for Ren to contradict her by saying, "*If* we get out of here," but for once, he took the hint and kept his mouth shut.

"You're also gonna need a shit ton of antibiotics and disinfectant treatment."

Really? I had to worry about this rubbish on top of staying alive and not losing a limb? Oh, Jesus. What if I had to get part of my back taken out like an amputation? I'm pretty certain that wasn't how it worked, but there's a first time for everything.

Even after Chess finished ripping up more of her shirt and wrapping it around my bloody skin, I didn't want to get up. I was fatigued, but it wasn't about that. I simply needed a moment to wallow in self-pity.

When we started this team, we agreed Ren was the hacker, Chess was the influencer, and I was the muscle. (That was only if we needed muscle. Otherwise I would just do whatever John wanted us to do.) Chess and Ren had their strengths, and physically they were mainly up to par. Well, Chess was. Ren was still up for assessment, but my battle with this physical journey was nothing but a disappointment. I could barely swim, Ren got heavy after a while even though he was roughly half my size, and if I needed to punch anyone soon, I would be lucky if they even flinched.

The rocky sand wasn't a comfortable platform to bury my face into, but it would only be a moment before I noticed something off. Or rather something I thought to be out of place. The smell. It was copper. Why would this tunnel be made out of copper? Was the *whole* thing made out of copper?

I probably received ghastly looks from Chess and Ren while scooping up the sand into my hands like drinking water from a lake, but I didn't care enough to notice. It was copper. I knew that smell anywhere. A sweaty metallic scent with a pinch of blood. But what was this color? The red and brown shade was much too dark and rich for normal copper.

"What?" I finally acknowledged Chess's voice.

"These aren't stones," I quietly responded. She wasn't surprised or confused. Neither was Ren. It was an answer. Not much of an answer, but it was a tiny cutout to a thousand-piece puzzle.

"What are they?" Ren asked.

"It's copper. But it's under-weight for copper and dark," I pointed out.

"Maybe it's mixed with something," Chess suggested. "And if that's true, we have one maniacal and patient alchemist hanging around."

"Maybe," I said even though it was the only possible explanation. What I couldn't explain was the familiarity of it all. The look, the tone, the vibrancy. I'd seen this material somewhere, but where?

There's a reason why we say, "It feels like it's been forever." That sense of time isn't just related to people. This was a recent finding. Whenever it was, I could still absorb the abstract ingredients standing out like a human in the jungle.

"I've got it," I mumbled. "I've seen this material before. Three times."

"Three times?" They both questioned.

"Yes. Once was the old man's pocket watch at the restaurant."

"Mr. Beau?" Chess asked. "How could he be involved?"

"Let me finish. The second was on the necklace of the old lady we sold a whole bunch of fake jewelry to. Remember that? I think that was a little over a month ago, and the third time was on the neck of the tiger. That's probably what was giving it magic."

It took a moment to register, but with a little reflection, Ren said, "That doesn't make any sense. Why would they - how would they be able to do any of this?"

Before I answered, I could see the work being done in Chess's eyes. A few more puzzle pieces were put together. She knew exactly what I was talking about.

"Because they're not involved," said Chess. "Whoever is doing this to us has been watching us a long time. They know our every move."

"Hopefully not all," I replied.

"Oh, please. They're probably listening in on us now."

I opened my mouth to respond, but as usual, the phenomenon of whispered hints continued as I was interrupted by the last voice that I wanted to hear.

"*Cruuush, crush, CRUSH, cruuush.*" My hearing was never top notch, but the voice was unquestionably increasing in volume. I only hoped that meant we were getting closer. Either that or I was gonna start shitting my pants soon.

"You heard a clue, didn't you?" Chess asked. Guess my face gave it away. "What did they say?"

"Crush?"

"Cute."

"Guess we'll just have to wait and figure out what the hell they mean," said Ren, "Whatever it is, it better come soon."

The two leaned their heads back on the wall opposite from me. If we were to get any more clues, they would probably figure this out eventually, but didn't want to tell them. Not only was this voice getting louder, the voice was becoming *clearer*. Like an upgrade from a nineties telly to a flat screen. Each whisper, each echo gave me an extra goosebump.

Over the next hour or so, I reviewed the flashing images of the pocket watch and necklace repeatedly. My obsession was already growing. Someone's lingering eyes had captured our private moments and knew personal information. At least my suspicions before were now debunked. It was all of us. Nobody was keeping any sort of life altering secret that would compromise the entire group. Although, my focus kept steering back towards John. Could he still be involved? I only wanted to know who we needed to call once we got out of this.

"We good to start walking again?" Chess asked.

"Yeah," Ren and I mumbled.

Everything stung. Not just my back, not just my head. My entire body. Dehydration and starvation did more than just eradicate your stomach and throat. We were dying, and it was starting to show.

"Anybody hear that?" Ren asked. I didn't, but I felt something. Almost like a car driving up behind you. The gentlest vibration, until it wasn't.

"Oh, you've got to be kidding me," Chess moaned. The last thing I wanted to do was agree with her, but I picked up what she put down. Another bloody earthquake.

17:
CHESS

Not only does vibration make me nauseous beyond repair, but it also gives me a nasty headache. So much so that my vision usually would give out. That's usually the gist of what happens during bad turbulence on airplane rides.

This was different. Something was off. This couldn't have been a normal earthquake. Earthquakes don't even last this long in California. It felt more like the rapid vibration of a phone. That's what we were. Just one giant phone, and someone refused to stop calling us.

"Everyone, close your eyes!" Paul instructed, because of course he did.

Trying not to have a stick too far up my ass, I followed his orders, but it was too late. Whatever water was in my stomach from drinking earlier, I for sure wasn't gonna be peeing it out anytime soon.

After throwing up and spitting out as much residue as I could, a loud crash came from right behind me. But when I turned around nothing was there. Then I heard it again. This time in front of me, but closer. I thought my head was gonna fall off if I whipped it around one more time.

"DUCK!" I heard Ren yell. Then it clicked. The freaking sky was falling. That was the whole point of this stupid earthquake. To crush us. The clue sounded more like a hint to the rocks rather than us, but thinking wasn't gonna go too smoothly with me in this condition.

"Wait!" I hollered. "Don't duck! We have to watch the rocks fall! We have to avoid them!" Take that, Paul.

The falling rocks were coming down faster and louder. I couldn't get a good look, but the rocks weren't breaking off from the roof of the tunnel. No. It would give us an escape route when they all came crashing down. They appeared out of nowhere. Materializing wherever they felt necessary, and vanishing the second they hit the floor. But best of all, they were most likely aiming for us.

"Get to the sides!" I screamed, plastering my body up against the wall of the cave. One insecurity I have is my anxiety over loud noises. God, I fucking hated them. All control was lost with the banging and pounding in my head and ears. My first instinct was to crouch down in a ball on the floor, but that would only create a larger target for the bombarding stones.

"Chess!" I heard, but I couldn't tell from who. "Chess!" Naturally I looked around to find the source of the screaming, while still covering my head with my shaking, intertwined fingers. But through the rocky, red shower and the bursting sand shooting into my eyes, I couldn't see either of them. "Chess! Ren's down!" Down? Oh no. If he was unconscious from cephalic impact there wasn't a lot I could do for him without water or drugs. But I had to try. I had to find them.

"PAUL?" I screamed. They must have been hiding in some sort of niche in the tunnel. Hovering my thumb over my eyebrows, as if I was blocking the sun, wasn't gonna do any good, but I did it anyway.

The prickling sand jabbed into every inch of my bare skin. If this stuff was toxic by consumption we were all dead. If I cracked my eyes open just a little bit, my skin glowed with a red tint mixed with the dust and just a little blood.

"PAUL? REN?"

Still nothing, but a speck of bravery surprisingly lifted my spirits and gave me the liberty to slide across the wall of the cave with my back still plastered to it. Although this sudden bravery could have easily been mistaken for fear.

"AHHH," I faintly heard. I didn't like that type of scream. Every type of scream was all too familiar with me as a nurse, but this one in particular was gruesome. The tightness in the throat usually implied it was extra painful, but you knew it was coming. Sometimes it was caused by the nurses due to necessary procedures, and believe me when I say; it was the second worst part of our jobs after seeing people … well, you know.

"AHHH," I heard it again. This time I was certain it was Paul. That wasn't good for two reasons. One: that meant Ren was still probably unconscious. Two: if Paul was now injured, there was no assistance for Ren. Especially if I couldn't get to them. Wait. No, make that three reasons. Now, I was responsible for two injured people. But here's the thing. If the screaming kept coming, it might give me a clue as to where they were. I just needed him to keep screaming, and as much as it pained me to say it, I needed him to scream louder.

"PAUL!"

I needed to start planning ahead. Even if I found them, and they were on the other side of the tunnel, how would I get to them? This heavy rainfall would knock me to my grave in seconds. It took me days to finally admit this, but it wasn't until this moment that I realized I was both afraid and hopeless, but I mainly felt hopeless. I didn't like being out of control in case that wasn't completely obvious.

I flirted with the idea of standing in the pounding precipitation by sticking my hand out in the open. A single rock the size of a tennis ball struck right smack in the middle of the back of my hand.

"FUCK!"

I thought I broke it, but after a few seconds of cradling it and shaking off the pain, the throbbing faded. How was I gonna do this? Well, there was only one answer, and I refused to accept that. The best I could do was cross my forearms over my head, and charge across to the other wall. It was, what? Eleven, twelve feet? I would be hit for sure, but it was the only way. If I held a rock above my head, another rock could fall on top of my protector and inertia would allow my head to be squashed.

Hold up.

Honestly, I was getting sick of these magical moments of realization, but an idea invaded my head. If I wanted to diminish something strong what would I do? Maybe crush it with a rock? Or more specifically, throw a rock at it. The only problem was, if I wanted to throw a rock at the tunnel wall, I would have to catch it. If it touched the ground, it would disappear.

Okay, okay, okay. More preparation was needed for this than jumping into a pool of water and swimming a hundred feet deep. *Just eyeball a smallish rock and cup your hands.* Easy enough, right?

The first few attempts were more than failures and more than pathetic. The rocks were avoiding me. I knew it. Just like their magnetism, following us wherever we went, if we tried to catch them, they would swerve away. Luckily, I was focused enough to detect their scheme. This could only mean I was on the right track.

Follow the swerve.

As stupid as it sounded, if I knew they were gonna bounce away from me, like two magnets pushing away from each other, I could snatch it at the last minute. These little shits, with minds of their own, would never see it coming. Whoever was behind this performance had creativity to admire, but we were going to beat them at their own game. After all, I got the hint that this person might have even *wanted* us to win.

First rock: flew right by me, and dodged in the opposite direction. Second rock: almost hit me in the face, but I was getting closer. Third rock: scraped my finger, and almost gave me a deep cut. Fourth rock: smacked right into the middle of my palms so quickly, I blinked, and it magically appeared.

I was on the t-ball field again. Eight years old, just caught the ball in the outfield for the first time ever. Only this time, I wasn't holding onto it for the rest of the game. My suppressed anger flew right out as I turned around to pound the rock right into the wall. My eyesight was still impaired, but right before me stood a hole. A hole the exact size of the rock I caught, and through that hole was light. What kind of light was it? I didn't know, but I refused to let any other option into my mind besides the option of daylight. Outside light. The light of freedom.

"PAUL!" I screamed once more. They had to be somewhere. There was a way out. If I couldn't find them, perhaps they already figured it out. Please. I prayed that was the truth.

"CHESS!" Like music to my ears. If that music was solely performed by a rock metal band and only consisted of an out-of-tune drum set.

"PAUL WHERE ARE YOU?" I almost coughed up a storm from opening my mouth so wide to scream.

"OVER HERE!" That wasn't helpful, but by chance I caught a glimpse of Ren's shiny black jacket across the tunnel to my left. "I CAN'T MOVE MY ARM! HE NEEDS HELP!" If my eyes weren't deceiving me, Paul was hunched down, holding his limp arm, trying to protect Ren who was laying on the ground. No time could be wasted. I had to get to them. Even if I yelled to Paul the directions on how to escape, he would need help dragging Ren out. Shit.

"I'M COMING!" I knew this type of fear. I couldn't put my finger on it exactly, but it was the picture-the-audience-in-their-underwear type of fear, but thank God it was, because that was the daring type that I liked. Although, I still hesitated.

What if I don't make it? What if Ren dies because of me?

No more thinking. Just...zoning. Centering myself so any type of fear wouldn't dare get in my way. A happy place. That's what I needed. Only one problem. My negative personality prevented me from ever making a committed decision as to where that would be. Fuji? Paris? Maybe, but something else came to mind, and it was risky as hell. Any day before my life went to shit. Before my life-altering mistake. Where not only I was my happiest, but when I felt the most myself. Where everything wasn't always great or smooth, but it was right. My life was right. Everything that I was doing was right. Pathetic, but the truth.

Okay, countdown. Three.

This was it.

Two.

My hands wouldn't stop sweating. The biggest chance of me dying so far, but what the hell.

One.

My feet never felt so numb, yet so alive and awake. Like they had a mind of their own. They shot away from the wall faster than my brain could even recognize that they already did. It was over in less than two seconds. I crouched down for just a second to cradle both of my arms that covered my head like the beasts that they are, but were already covered in bruises and blood. Then, in a flash, one of the bigger rocks struck me in the back and caused me to fall over.

Staying down wasn't an option. I would get hit again in a second or less, but the pain was worse than my allergic reaction a few days ago. Besides, becoming paralyzed was the second to last thing I needed at the moment. Death was of course in first place.

No matter the pain, I fought through it and stuck my back to the wall, ready to find the boys. The damages to my arms didn't stop them from doing their jobs of protecting my head and face. Just in case more demonic stones wanted to attack me again.

"Chess!" Paul hollered in my ear as he grabbed me. My heart jumped a beat. He must have seen me coming and managed to pull Ren towards me.

"The rocks can break down the wall!"

"What?"

"THE ROCKS CAN BREAK DOWN THE WALL!" He heard me, but still didn't seem to understand. "Catch one!"

We would need to catch more than one. Actually, we caught four before we even saw a single hole in the wall. I guess this side wasn't as sunny as the other.

Time was running short. Not because of Ren, but because the rocky storm was getting heavier and heavier, because why wouldn't it? Just another catch to finding new information.

"Come on!" I said after deciding the hole was big enough. Freedom and safety were so close. Maybe not total safety. We still were hella dehydrated and starved for God's sake, but no more tunnel. UV rays and overcoming darkening depression was at the tip of my finger.

Paul shoved Ren out of the hole first, then himself. I was the last, which thank God I was, because I don't think Paul would have handled getting knocked out and falling out of the hole, instead of crawling, as well as I did.

The ceiling came crumbling down harder and harder the second we began our exit, but as my right foot stepped in after my left, that was the least of my concerns. I've always been a klutz, but after I fell face first onto the sandy floor right outside the tunnel, I immediately regretted not moving faster when I came face to face with a black, rotting skeleton that looked like it had been there for over a hundred years.

"AHHHHH!" I screamed louder than I had this entire journey. I couldn't point out exactly where I was at that point, but now it looked like a replica of the original tunnel, only darker and with more grueling spirits haunting my soul.

The strength to stand up hadn't aroused yet. Although my arms found the energy to scurry away from the emo mummy until I ran into another one.

"AHHHHH!" I knew it was pointless, but I couldn't stop screaming. I didn't see a way out. I was trapped. Even worse, my eyes quickly adjusted to the darkness. I didn't have time to notice if there was a deathly smell that could kill me at any moment. I was too busy being entranced by the horror of the hundreds of bones and skeletons that covered the entire floor of the tunnel.

What was there to do? Destroying my vocal chords and crouching in the corner seemed like the only option, so it was the option that I went with.

"No, no, no, no, no." My eyes never squeezed shut so tightly before. Normally if I was ever scared, my eyes would stay wide open, so I wouldn't miss a damn thing. This time was different. I knew exactly what was happening, but I couldn't bear to watch. I stayed that way until my head slammed against a giant boulder, or at least I think that's what it was. The impact forced me to open my eyes to see the images of skeletons fading away into oblivion. What the replacing image was, I couldn't tell, but it was bright. The last thing I remembered passing through my mind was the last thing I wanted to realize; the absence of two men that were supposed to be by my side this whole time, and not leave me high and dry.

"Paul? Ren?" I mumbled as my vision, once again, blurred and my voice dropped three octaves.

Oh no, not again.

18:
PAUL

It didn't make any sense. Where the hell was I? I mean I knew I was outside, but that escape was way too easy, but of course being upset about escaping a tunnel that was trying to kill you was rather irrational. All around me was fresh air, wind, and light. I was free. *We* were free. My arm felt like I got bit by five snakes at one time, but I guess that was the price of freedom. I didn't care about what I said about our initial intentions for when we got out. I just wanted to experience the moment and acknowledge our freedom for as long as I could.

When watching a film about freedom, people always recite these rubbish monologues about how they noticed the beauty in their surroundings more than they usually did before. I didn't do that for a moment. Everything looked exactly as beautiful as it always had. I took in the normality of my surroundings. Right as it should be. The cloudy blue sky, the patchy green grass that definitely needed watering. All back to its regular schedule.

Bugger, I almost forgot how badly I needed food. Where was the closest Wendy's? But hold on...where were Chess and Ren? How was I just noticing this now? Oh, bloody hell. Seriously?

"Chess? Ren?" I called out, in a field, in the middle of nowhere. I didn't have any other strategies in my back pocket. "CHESS? REN?" I yelled a little louder a few more times. "YOU'VE GOT TO BE JOKING, RIGHT?"

"Bloody hell, Paul," I heard Ren say right behind me, mocking my accent, which he never did. "We're right here. There's no need to yell."

Both Ren and Chess approached me as if nothing was wrong, but their excitement about being out of the tunnel evidently showed in their voices and faces.

"You guys alright?" I asked them.

"Why wouldn't we be? We're out!" Chess hollered, jumping around doing an awkward dance with her hips.

"What about you?" Ren asked, looking at me with his weary eyes. "What do you want to do right at this very moment? Any requests?"

I had a lot of requests. I wanted to learn how to play the piano, I wanted to go cliff diving. Hell, I even wanted to go to Disney World. But my eyebrows involuntarily knit, confused as to why they weren't as desperate for food as I was.

"I think the best thing for us to do right now is go get food," I told them. "Why don't we start walking? Maybe there's something along that road over there." There was no objection before we walked the pathway my finger directed towards. Only smiling faces. Overly bright smiling faces.

The road wasn't about to have any tourist attractions for miles, let alone restaurants. Maybe a pit-stop, or a convenience store, but the lack of pavement on the dirt roads implied we were in a different state and possibly a different hemisphere. Home was nowhere to be found.

"What type of food are you two hoping for?" I asked them.

"Ice cream," Chess answered. "Lots and lots of ice cream." I was about to ask her which flavor until I remembered Chess saying something about her inability to eat dairy a few months ago, but then again, it was Chess. The last person I knew to bide by many rules even if they were scientifically difficult to fight against.

"I think I'll have some Cheez-Its," said Ren. Strange choices for their first meal in days, but who was I to argue?

"I'm about to scarf down a double cheeseburger," I told them. "I don't care from where. I just need meat in my body."

The fact that we could all still stand and walk was a miracle. I'd never gone this long without some form of pig or cow passing through my intestines. I'm sure Chess could say the same thing about red wine.

I'd never been so happy to breathe such dry air. Although, there was something about the environment that was unsettling. Perhaps my gut was telling me I wasn't going to find any food ahead of me, or maybe it was because I kept seeing the same tree to the left of me with a broken branch right in the middle of the trunk. Either my eyes were playing tricks on me or someone else was playing tricks on me. Chess or Ren would know. Actually, maybe just Chess would know.

"Hey, you two," I called out to them after a long silence. "You guys notice anything weird? Like something is off?"

"Why would you ask that?" Chess asked.

"Don't laugh at me, because I know we've been walking in a straight line for a while, but I feel like we're walking in circles."

After a beat of silence and an exchange of muted smiles, the two burst into laughter like two bank robbers who escaped unharmed.

"What are you talking about?" Ren asked. "You literally just said it yourself. You know we've been walking in a straight line. We have to keep walking. We will find food eventually. Or at least before you need a long nap."

If the laughter wasn't obvious enough, I knew he was poking fun at me, but to be fair he was right. Immediately after stuffing food in my face, I was surely going to sleep for three days minimum. I hadn't looked in a mirror for a few days either, but I must have looked like I was so beyond sleep deprived that I would go to the top of the list for a heart transplant without any real tests.

I managed to ignore them for the next couple of hours. They were hungry and sleep deprived too. I couldn't give them too hard of a time. What we really needed to do was find out where the hell we were. Even if John was involved in this, he didn't know we suspected him. Perhaps he could still be of some use, and if we - *Oh wow*. I didn't think of checking my phone until that very moment. Weird.

"Do your phones work?" I asked, trying to find mine and praying the water hadn't completely damaged it.

"Um," Chess mumbled. "I don't know, let me check." She didn't know where her phone was either, but here was the difference; I've never been attached to my phone. Chess, being about ten years younger than I, always knew where her phone was. She would be the last person to ever lose it. "Oh, right. Jacket pocket." But she only said that after she found it, instead of actually recalling where it was. "Nope, not working."

"Mine isn't working either," said Ren.

Even weirder. My phone wasn't just working, it was fully charged. But unfortunately, no signal. But I'm no nutter, so I kept this information to myself hoping to use it against them. How would I do that? No idea, but just in case.

We travelled on, mainly in silence while I occasionally peaked at my phone, searching for service, but nothing. Not even one bar for half a second.

Every ten minutes or so, I saw that same damn tree. After maybe the twentieth time, my gaze would linger so long I convinced myself it was staring straight back at me. Or maybe it was screaming at me, trying to tell me something.

Trying to tell me something, but what?

The horrifying proposition ran through my brain, and no matter how hard I tried, I couldn't kick it out. The moment Chess and Ren appeared out of nowhere, they'd been completely different. They still displayed their usual characteristics, but they weren't acting like I expected them to. But if they were in on this from the beginning, why didn't they just kidnap or kill me now? Or worse, what if they were leading me to the money only to rip it from me and run away with it?

No. That couldn't be it. Why would John request this betrayal from Chess *and* Ren? Wouldn't he ask just one of them? Again, no! He would have asked me before asking either of them. Or maybe he would ask Chess or me, but why Ren?

Still, I could have had it all wrong. It was time to ask some questions. Interrogation would lead me deeper into this mystery.

"So," I tried to say as casually as possible. "After we get a hold of John, where do we want to go? We absolutely need a holiday, or just a break from work. Somewhere that will make us forget any of this happened."

This was my strategy; get them to blabber on and hope they slip up on what they were planning on doing next. But if I were to get any information out of them, there was about to be a slippery slide right into what would look like mindless banter.

"What about London?" Ren asked. "I've always wanted to go." To be fair, Ren repeated, and in detail, his desire to visit London, even though that city gave me minor P.T.S.D. Which I repeatedly, and in detail, told him about.

"I like Cambridge better. Why not there?" I suggested.

"Paul," Chess chimed in. "Don't be lame. We gotta go visit the Queen before she dies. I bet she's really eager to meet us."

"Hilarious." What else could I ask before the mood died? "I've got it! Miami." My hands slapped together as if I had just won the pub quiz. "Ren, you said you love it there. And don't you have family there? Let's visit. Have a few laughs. Go to the beach. Visit your Aunt Sophie?" Ren had told me once that his parents were only children. He had no aunts or uncles.

But before Ren could answer, Chess opened her big mouth and answered for him by saying, "Nahhhh." She almost sounded drunk at this point. Bloody hell she needed water. "I'd rather go to nice beaches. There are some amazing ones in Santa Barbara that I could show you guys."

My slapstick double take wasn't too obvious considering it was just my ears filling with confusion. Chess's Santa Barbara was my London. We never wanted to return there. Unless of course, we wanted our haunting suicidal thoughts to follow us through our journeys.

"Really?" I asked, hoping to get more out of her. "You wanna go back there?"

"You know...why not?" As if there was nothing to lose any more. She completely took a 180 and changed her mind. I must say, not what I was expecting.

I didn't mean to, but my feet stuck to the ground while the other two kept walking.

"Who are you two?" I heard myself say.

"What was that?" Ren asked. Something sly in his voice rippled from not only his lips, but his eyes. There was no going back now.

"What have you done with Chess and Ren?" It had to be true. Without an ounce of hesitation, they confirmed my suspicions.

"I really wish you hadn't said that, Paul," said Chess. It wasn't the first part of that sentence that made me run away at full speed. It was the fact that Chess called me "Paul", and not "dude" or "fucker" or something American like that. I sure as hell didn't know where I was going, but I wasn't free. Quickly, I accepted that. I had to. As I sprinted past that same lameass tree, I realized that this was some other version of the tunnel. That's why the road was straight and never ending. God, I was one thick bastard.

"Paul!" I heard Chess scream out. She couldn't have been too far behind me. "You can't just run forever. There is a limit, you know?" I didn't know what the hell that thing was talking about, and I didn't care. Were they demons? Were they being possessed? Well, shit. If they were being possessed, that meant I couldn't hurt them.

"Paul!" Apparently now it was Ren's turn to repeatedly call out my name. "You have nothing to be afraid of, you know? What could we possibly do to you?" Again, didn't wanna know. All I wanted to do was reach the small patch of woods, and I was almost there, just a few more meters.

"Oh, look!" Chess screamed out with full abdominal support. Their ability to yell and run after me at the same time made me lean more toward the demon option. "He's heading into the woods."

"How do you expect to get out of this, Paul?" That right there was something I *did* have to care about, but I needed more time, and hiding behind a tree for as long as I could without making any noise would hopefully give me just that.

19:
REN

Sometimes, when we read, our minds can drift off into space for a whole page but still manage to keep our eyes skimming across the paper. That's what this part of the journey was like. Flashes of my surroundings crashed upon me, but I couldn't fully piece it together. Mainly because I didn't know what was going on. The last thing that I remembered was breaking through the ceiling of the cave, but feeling no sigh of relief. (Mainly because I was unconscious.) And even though I could see we escaped and were in the city of Atlanta once again, I had yet to breathe in the air of freedom. I still couldn't point out why.

"Guys," Chess yelled, beckoning us as we all ran in unison. "This way." What we were running towards was still unclear, but I was too distracted by my shock and puzzlement with our change of scenery. How were we still in Atlanta? "Get in."

It was my car. My beautiful, almost new, black, mom van parked right in front of a gas station. Wait. *Gas station?*

"We ready to get the hell outta here?" Paul asked, buckling up.

"Yes, but, where are we?" I responded.

"Doesn't matter, you nutter!" Paul's delirious laugh gave me no comfort in our safety. "We're going home. That's all that matters." The shoulder squeeze he gave me was a gorilla grip as usual. Something felt right, but everything else felt off, and I was still too entranced in my daze to figure out what it was.

"Where are we going?"

"Why all of the freaking questions?" Chess asked, putting the car into drive.

"Wait, why is Chess driving? She hates driving."

"Again!" Her voice popped like a jack-in-the-box. "Why all the questions?"

"Okay, fine. Just one more." I could hear Chess's eyes roll to the back of her head, but I proceeded to annoy her anyway. "Can we go through a drive thru?"

"Now, that we can do," Paul laughed.

"What are we feeling?" Chess asked, but I could barely pay attention to what she was saying, considering my car was straddling the double yellow line like a strip club dancer.

"Chess," I stuttered. "Can you slow down? I don't want you to mess up Vanessa."

Paul looked at me as if I was about to throw up on his shoes. "Mate, you named your car?"

"Doesn't everyone?" A genuine question, really. "Anyway, it doesn't matter where we go. I just need food."

"Your words, not mine," said Chess. What was that supposed to mean? Were we going to a slaughter house and eating the meat fresh off the table? I suppose questioning Chess's odd intentions was something I should have dropped a while ago, but still. Something about her slow, spiteful tone made me squirm in my seat.

"Alright." Something about my environment made me feel out of control. It wasn't that I didn't try to hide my discontent, it's that I couldn't. The words slipped out of me and even after they were dispersed, I still couldn't fully process the conversation.

"So, when are we going after John?" Chess asked.

"Why would we be going after John?"

"Hello?" Her voice contained a hint of more valley girl energy than usual. "We need to go beat his ass for throwing us in hell! I bet he didn't expect us to get out. I can't wait to see the look on his face when he sees we've escaped. Although I'm way more anxious to see the look on his face when we kick his ass. Or - when Paul and I kick his ass."

"Oh, right. We're still on that." I almost hoped she didn't hear that, but I couldn't care. The only thing that I needed more than food, and for Chess to shut up for once, was to sleep. Come to think of it, letting Chess drive wasn't so bad after all. *Damn, did I really just say that?*

"Before we knock him out, we gotta make sure we know who else was involved," Paul added. "They might still be after us."

"Good idea. More asses to kick," Chess's sudden comfort in violence was way too casual in my opinion.

Dropping down across the back seat, my eyes went back and forth between the back of my eye lids and the roof of my car.

109

Each detail, whether big or small, crawled into my vision as both dazed and sharp at the same time. But my strongest sense caused me to perk up and sniff the smell of Burger King passing us.

"Hey," I snapped. "We just passed Burger King. Why didn't you pull over?"

"You said wherever, right?" Chess asked, without turning her head to look at me.

"That's not what I meant." I meant to raise my voice. I did, but the rage wouldn't rise to the level I needed it to.

"Just let us take care of things," Paul butted in. Oh, so he was in on this too? Why weren't they as desperate for food as I was? With my deprivation from everything, I was on my deathbed. How did they have so much energy?

A few slow minutes went by, or at least I thought they did, before Chess finally said, "Here we are!" Right before me stood the biggest, brightest, Wendy's I had ever seen.

"Finally!" Until now, I hadn't realized how drenched in saliva my mouth was. A heart attack on a plate never looked so good.

"Yeah I'll get three cheeseburgers and three cokes. Make mine a diet!" Weird. First of all, Chess thought it would be funny to order with a slight Southern accent. Second, she hated soda. Especially diet soda. Something about her seeing too many patients with rotting teeth.

"Here ya go, mate," said Paul, handing me my food.

"Yes, yes, yes, ye-" My mouth stopped mid word when I took one look at my burger, if that's what you could call it. The circumference ran a third of the size of any other burger in America and the bun sat as flat as a pancake. "Where's the rest of it?"

"What are you talking about?" Chess asked, taking a bite into her burger which was three times the size of, you guessed it, Any. Other. Burger. In. America.

"Can I at least have my drink?" I'm not sure why that was my next concern, but I couldn't stop the words from escaping my lips.

"Sure!" Paul responded, overly excited, but his fake excitement immediately vanished when he dropped my soda right onto the backseat floor. "Oops!"

His fingers wiggled against his fake laugh as my jaw dropped straight into the drenched floor. *My caaaaar.*

Screw the soda. Poor Vanessa didn't deserve this, and these two idiots didn't seem to care. No. Scratch that. They definitely didn't care.

"Can we go somewhere else?" I asked, eating my slider in one bite.

"Ren," Chess moaned, completely turning around while driving. "Why can't you be more appreciative of everything? We do so much for you!"

"Chess! Watch out!" Not even a flinch escaped her. The oncoming truck veered out of the way while Chess's eyes still punctured my soul. She was going to kill us, but my mouth couldn't form the words to tell her that.

"Is there a problem, Renny?" She had never called me that before. Usually my nicknames were *idiot*, *dumbass*, or *loser*. Chess was probably one of the popular girls in high school.

"No. I just need food."

"More? Ughhh." How small did she think I was? I thought being five foot seven and having a little beer gut would be enough to get at least a decent salad.

"Please just stop anywhere." Again, I didn't mean to say that. Why couldn't I fully control my side of the conversation? I wasn't dreaming. If I was, I wouldn't be shivering with hunger, but it was almost as if I was *watching* a dream.

"Are you sure you want that?" Paul asked.

"More than anything. Trust me."

Chess finally turned around, got comfortable in her chair and said, "Man, the things we do for you."

20:
CHESS

One of the rocks must have knocked me out. Either that or I was having a brain hemorrhage. Or maybe both. Goodie me. But the first thing I remembered was the burning in my eyes. Sleeping in the sunlight is never healthy, but waking up to it is pure torture. All I wanted was to go back to being unconscious, and find the switch to turn off the sun. But when I didn't see either Ren or Paul right next to me, that didn't seem like the best option.

"Guys?" I croaked, still laying on my back. No response. The blood dripping from my forehead was the only form of life that I felt present. Then I thought, *Oh yeah, I've already done this. Right before I passed out...again.*

I should have been elated. I was outside. There were trees and open land to walk on everywhere I looked. I was alive. I was *free*, but without a single doubt I was not safe. The worst part; I had no idea what was endangering me.

Nothing else felt broken as I worked my way back up to sitting. Standing was coming soon, but not for another twenty minutes. Only a few bruises and scrapes besides my forehead. Maybe the boys were right behind me. Maybe they went to look for help and would come back for me. Even if that wasn't the case, I needed food. I prayed to God there were some berries or something in the woods a few feet away from me. Either that or I was about to get eaten by a bear, but honestly either one would put me out of my misery, so I wasn't picky.

The fresh air somehow rejuvenated my body just enough so I could walk without passing out. Even better, I couldn't smell my wretched body odor as badly. The third thing I was gonna do, once I could, after eating a bucket of french fries and drinking the entire Atlantic Ocean, was take a bubble bath that was so hot, I wouldn't have any skin left.

Still no sign of the boys. They probably left me. I didn't blame them. Don't get me wrong, if that was actually the case I would have been pissed. But let's be real, I would have done the same thing. We've already saved each other countless times. We didn't owe each other anything. Although, if they did leave me to go off and look for food, they were about to miss the bomb ass blueberries I spotted.

"Oh shiiiit," I didn't even know blueberries grew in this part of the country, and I didn't give it a single thought as I chowed down on the worst, driest, oldest blueberries I ever put in my mouth. But they were delicious. Anything would have been delicious at this point.

Maybe a hundred dried up berries hung from that bush, but they were all gone within roughly forty-seven seconds. All except one. The last tiny berry came about an inch away from my mouth before something in the woods startled me so abruptly I dropped it.

Snap!

Something or someone was following me. The feeling of jeopardy approached me once again, while Ren and Paul were still nowhere to be found. I was still alone, and I've never done alone well.

Snap!

They were getting closer. The birds rippled away, afraid of the sound. Oh, how I wish I was one of those goddamn birds. Flying away from your problems sounded like the best mode of transportation.

Snap!

Odd. This time it came from the other side of me. Oh no, there were two of them. Maybe even more. I was outnumbered.

I've got it. The tree right next to me looked like a piece of cake. A four-year-old could climb it. A very tall four-year-old, but still. Maybe if I went quickly, they wouldn't notice where I went.

"Okay, okay," I whispered before I realized that I really needed to shut up and get going. My sore and weak muscles gained just enough adrenaline to form a perfect squat that would release me straight into the air and wrap my arms around the first trunk. One leg over. No problem. Other leg over? Problem. But the adrenaline wouldn't stop.

The bark pierced into my skin, unwilling to slow down. Each fiber in my bicep felt like it was about to explode. My stomach crept upon the top of the trunk. Just a few inches away, but the adrenaline wasn't enough anymore. I needed pure strength, and clever skills.

Just when I thought I was gonna plunge to the ground and disclose my location, my free foot pushed against a smaller branch that gave me just enough leverage to regrip both of my hands over the trunk. With my stomach and chest now flat on the trunk, I was safe and secure. No one would find me if I just kept climbing. Besides, the rest of the branches were closer together. Easy.

"Alright, get up," I told myself. My bleeding hands crawled closer to my crotch, causing me to stand up and see a dark silhouette of a human being five feet away from me, sitting on the branches, reflecting me.

"AHHH!" I didn't mean to scream. I really didn't. But I lost control, and with losing control of my vocal chords and the rest of my body, I teetered over that branch so fast, there wasn't any time to have my life flash before my eyes.

My jeans ripped fiber by fiber along that bark. That's all I could address before I appeared in someone's arms down below. Or maybe it was two sets of arms.

"Chess?" I heard Ren say with my eyes still closed.

"You alright?" Paul added.

"Uh -" I mean, I was, but was I? "Yeah, I'm fine. Where were you two?"

"What do you mean?" Ren laughed, which he usually never did. "Looking for you!" He adopted a sinister laughter that should have twisted my stomach in knots, but it didn't, and I couldn't point out why.

"Oh, yeah o' course," I laughed along. "Let's get outta here. Sorry, I ate all of the berries that were over here. Let's go get food."

"Sick," said Paul, which he never said.

I took a moment to find relief and peace for the first time in the past few days. Not a cloud in the sky, I made it out alive. Regardless of my insecurities, I was okay, but the more I thought about it, something else was bothering me. "Where are we anyway?"

"Santa Barbara."

I froze. My feet sunk to the ground. My face didn't look scared or angry, just blank. How? How could they do this to me? I didn't cry very often, but the amount of anxiety that rushed to my forehead in a matter of two seconds almost made me pass out.

"Why?" I asked. "How did we end up here?" My cracking voice couldn't resist the anger. It might not have been them, but someone was out to get me, still.

"You don't think it's some sort of message?" Paul asked.

"What kind of message is this? I don't wanna be here!" Stupidly, my feet regained control and ran in the complete opposite direction. Something was telling me I needed to get away from these people, but these people were my guys. Unless...

"Where you goin'?" Fake Ren magically hopped right in front of me before I could really get anywhere. I was trapped. Fake Paul on one side, Fake Ren on the other.

"Look, whoever told you to do this -" They both burst into uncontrollable, cartoonish laughter.

"Chessy, honey. Since when do we take orders from other people?" I didn't answer. It barely registered as a question in my brain.

I managed to fit in a few steps towards Fake Ren. He usually felt a little intimidated by me. "What did they do to you?"

No answer.

There were only two possibilities here. Either they were captured and altered in some way while I was unconscious, or these people weren't Ren or Paul. But I knew one thing; if either of them were going to attack me, there wasn't any room for mercy. I would just have to deal with the consequences later.

"Is something wrong, Chess?" Fake Paul asked.

"No," I said, casually. "Why would there be?" If I played their game, whatever that game was, would they leave me alone? What was the goal on this level? And how the living fuck would I pass it?

"Then why won't you come with us to Santa Barbara?"

They weren't taking me to Santa Barbara. Wherever we were, it wasn't real. All of this had to be an illusion, or at least all of my surroundings. Ren and Paul could be holograms for all I knew. But wherever we were going had to be a trap. Or, what if staying put was the trap? Holy shit, I was giving myself a headache.

"Why don't I catch up with you guys later and meet you there?" Well that was a stupid thing to say, but it was commit or eat shit, right? "I think it'll be best for me to stay here for a while, but I promise on my life I will meet you guys there." On my life? Oh God, this wasn't gonna work. What was I saying? And why couldn't I stop this shit from pouring out of my mouth like a waterfall?

"That wasn't on our list of instructions." I couldn't tell you who said that. It sounded more like Paul, but I blacked out before I noticed. I didn't feel any pain before I lost consciousness, but perhaps that's because this place was as fake as my mother's nose. I woke up, only God knows how long afterwards, with another throbbing headache. I wondered how much more of this I could handle until I was permanently brain damaged.

"Wha-?" Now my throat was too dry to talk. I didn't think it was possible to be even more dehydrated than before, but hey, what fun would that be?

After a few minutes of fading in and out, I grasped a hold of my fingertips and toes first before I could control every muscle in all four of my limbs. And to my surprise, (I still honestly don't know why this was a surprise) both my hands and feet were cuffed. Both individually bolted to the metal platform I was plastered to. Why? Where the hell did they get freaking CUFFS?

"I wouldn't scream if I were you," Fake Paul whispered in the corner.

My eyes focused on him for just a moment before I gathered up the words, "You're not real."

"How do you know that?" He jumped towards me and deepened his voice. I never knew it could go so low.

"Where's Ren?"

"Why do you ask?" Fake Ren asked as he magically appeared out of nowhere, right over my goddamn head.

"What the-? What's your problem?" I would have scrunched into a little egg if I could.

"Chess, sweetheart." I hated people calling me that, and he knew that too. I guess these fake versions of my colleagues knew enough to try and brainwash me, but I found it amusing they thought they were going to. "What is it exactly that makes you so afraid of Santa Barbara?"

Was he serious? "Ohhhh." I couldn't help but maniacally laugh. It wouldn't scare them, but it wouldn't scare me either. "So, that's what this is about? Whoever is trying to kill us in that tunnel wants me to face my fears? Is that right?"

Seriously. Was this a crime show about a serial killer obsessed with fear? That shit had been done way too many times.

"Not exactly," said Fake Paul, curling the ends of his mouth. "I'd say it's more about putting you in a vulnerable position. Therefore, you can be used in whatever way is useful."

"Yeahhh," I slurred. "'Cause that makes perfect sense."

"You might not get it now." No shit. "But wait until you see your real friends again. You'll see what we're talking about."

"So, you're saying I'll make it out of here, and onto the next level, alive?" The words slipped out before I could stop them. Maybe that wasn't the smartest thing to say. I couldn't let myself be at a disadvantage.

"That'll be up to you."

Who the hell were these people? Were they even people? Not important. I needed to find a clue. Who knew if that bitch was gonna whisper anything to me. She didn't last time I was alone. The only thing I could do right now was look around for anything that could help me and keep these boys talking, and I knew just how to do that.

"What are you guys getting in return for this?" To be honest, I still wasn't even sure if these guys were human, but there must have been some source of life inside them that was programmed to respond to specific conversations.

"Why do you want to know?" Fake Paul answered.

"I just wanna know how long you've been down here and such. Are you guys trapped too? Are you gonna be free once you do this?"

Both of them laughed, but it was an easy laugh. The sort of laugh that says, "I'm used to being asked this."

"There are so many things about this place that you don't want to know anything about," said Fake Ren.

"What sort of things?"

"Why do you ask so many questions?" No more laughter. Nothing but annoyance now. It was unexplainable, but something stabbed into me and told me I was on the right track.

"Maybe it has something to do with me being handcuffed to...I don't even know...is this a coffee table?"

"You think you're really smart, don't you?" Fake Ren asked.

"Smart? You're joking, right?" That wasn't completely true. Sometimes I was a fucking genius, but Fake Ren couldn't have any hold over me. It was working, and these idiots gave it all away. They wanted me to be vulnerable. So, I would be, because they didn't think I was strong enough to be. Idiots. But I was gonna do it my way.

"You're sad, aren't you?" I asked Fake Paul. "Are you even real?" Okay, I didn't mean to ask that so transparently, but it worked.

"Sad?" he responded. "Why would you ask that? And I told you to stop asking so many questions."

"No. You asked me why I asked so many questions. You never said -" But he cut me off by snapping what looked like his belt on my arm.

"Jesus! Why don't you ever shut up?" Paul Screamed.

"Again, are you joking?"

"JUST SHUT UP!"

"AHHH!" I didn't even see the knife in his hand before it slammed into my forearm. I knew Paul was strong, but shit. I would have kicked him if my legs contained more energy. The pain didn't last for long. It probably wasn't supposed to. Another sign that I was leading myself the right way.

They thought I couldn't feel like a human being anymore. This wasn't about emotional fear. All they cared about was the fear of pain. Physical, bloody pain.

"I'd listen to him if I were you," said Fake Ren. I was listening alright. It was working. I was playing their game.

"Believe me," I squealed. "My ears are wide open. But what about you? Both of you. Aren't you afraid?"

Fake Paul wiped off the blood from his knife in an almost seductive way and said, "And what would we have to be afraid of?"

118

"Are you afraid of me?" That caught them off guard. Paul's nose twitched with surprise, but no anger. Patiently, I waited, but he only left his eyes on me making me more uncomfortable than earlier. He asked this question before. Many times, but my response was new to him, and he was enjoying every minute of it.

He was gonna let me go. I was going on to the next level. Or at least that's what I thought until his knife plunged into my arm once again.

"Wha - Ah!" This time was different. He carved something into my arm, but I had to look away. I had to keep screaming. "Ahhh! WHAT ARE YOU DOING?"

"Chessy," Fake Paul whispered, still cutting me up. "Stay still and everything will go as planned."

I barely took in what he said. The chill of the blade faded once he finished, but I was still cold, and the warm blood dripping down my arm didn't help.

"And by the way," said Fake Paul. Instead of wiping off the blade this time, he gave it one big snap before he grabbed my bloody arm. "Keep making people afraid of you. You'll survive longer." One by one, his fingers released me. I expected there to be more blood than there was, but because of that, my weary eyes caught sight of the most peculiar thing.

FALL.

Letter by letter, in all caps, dug into my forearm. The next clue. Creative.

How was I gonna get this to the boys? Did they have it too? Even if they did, I couldn't risk it, and there was only one way that they could possibly hear me. Literally.

"FAAAAALL!" I screamed. The fake boys didn't do anything. Not even a single blink. "FAAAAALL!"

21:
PAUL

Maybe ten minutes passed. I measured based on my pulse. About three beats per second, and it wasn't going down anytime soon. I still don't know how such a large man could run so quietly over crunchy, dry leaves. My only worry was that they'd been watching me this whole time. Laughing at my gullible, oblivious personality.

The more I moved around, hiding behind the trees, the more exposed I felt. Like standing naked in front of an open window.

One tree was perfect to hide in. The niche in the trunk was big enough to hide bigfoot and me at the same time. Not only that, but it was perfect for shade. The longer I was outside, the faster my insides boiled. Taking off my jacket wasn't an option. If I abandoned it, they could trace me. If I held it in my hands, it would make more noise. Dehydrated perspiration it will be.

The second the back of my head hit the tree trunk I couldn't help but agonize. *When will this end?* In all truthfulness, I didn't care anymore. I didn't want to know why this was happening to us. I simply wanted it to end. If this was karma, I was willing to swear on my life never to do anything dishonest again. The future wasn't what I was worried about. Why would it be? I had money. All three of us had money. We would be fine. If I didn't know who was behind this for the rest of my life I would sleep like a baby every goddamn night.

"Please," I whispered under my breath. "Please. I'll do anything."

"Really?" Chess's voice came out of nowhere. "I find that hard to believe."

Somehow, I wasn't startled. Afraid, yes, but not startled. The two imposters stood before me as I opened my eyes. "And what makes you say that?"

"Well, it's not that I don't think you'll do anything. I've seen what you eat after all. But you have standards, don't you?"

"This entire journey has been about sacrifices."

"No!" Chess bolted forward, inches away from my face. "It's been about weakness, and negligence. And you're not gonna make it through if you don't know that."

"Is that what you think?"

"What are you talking about?" Ren asked.

"Do you think you're weak and neglected?" Honestly, I wasn't sure what I was asking, but the word vomit continued, and somewhere in my brain it made sense.

"This place isn't about us," said Chess.

"I wouldn't be so sure." Thinking they wouldn't attempt an attack just yet, I stood up with shaky legs, hoping the advantage of my height would overpower them. "You're the barrier between me and the next level in this little game, but they expect me to succeed. That's what games are supposed to be about, right? The ringmaster wants there to be a winner. That means you two are supposed to be...well...weak? I don't make the rules, sweetheart."

I never called Chess *sweetheart* before, and thank God I never did. Because the punch that dug right into my face next was much stronger than expected.

Luckily, I wasn't completely thrown off balance. My shaky leg still managed to kick her in the stomach, while my elbow cracked Ren's windpipe. I didn't have much time, but my feet started up once again, dashing at a speed I didn't know I could reach. Hiding wasn't gonna do anything besides stall my escape. I had to keep moving, and somehow, I knew that meant leaving the woods.

Keep going, keep going, I thought over and over again until I stopped doubting myself. My legs, my arms, my core all started disintegrating, but my heart refused to let me down. Every ounce of strength that dropped, my heart only compensated for it.

I knew it was stupid, but I repeatedly and impulsively looked behind me to see no one following me. Where were they? What if they knew where I was going? That would be absurd considering I didn't even know where I was going, but I couldn't rule it out. Still, even after I convinced myself to keep my head forward, no footsteps or heavy breathing was to be heard besides mine.

Beads of sweat stuck to my forehead and chest. Finally, some basic science in here that I could understand. I hated running without music, so to my regret, this was my point of focus to distract me from the physical burden.

Please cool me off, sweat. A great place to be at in life.

An end to the woods was near. Just a few meters away from me. Of course, the sun shined brighter with no shade, but I would survive.

The shin splints crept in from around the corner, but manageable so far. I was honestly surprised my shins had lasted this long.

"Come on, come on." I still don't know which part of my body I was talking to, but my stomach needed it most at this moment. The empty hole cried in anger, and there was nothing I could do.

The first step out of the woods rang with freedom. It took me a while to realize why that was. I still wasn't to safety, but something about the bright, sunset view reminded me that there was somewhere to go. Some place without danger.

For some reason the back of my head convinced me that I needed to look back, just one more time. Once more. That's all I needed. A bit of rubbish if you asked me, but my tingling senses told me it was the strategic and smart choice to make, and my subconscious and I hate arguing, so why not?

If someone was watching me and they blinked, they would have missed my head snapping around to check my surroundings. Not a soul in sight. I must admit, I was worried before I confirmed my temporary safety, but in just a flash that disappeared.

"Whoa!" If I took one step further, I would have fallen off a cliff. A deep, foggy, echoing cliff. The type horses jump off in films, praying they would land on the other side.

My heart had been beating in my throat for some time, but now I thought both my neck and chest were about to explode at the same time.

Where did this come from? How was I seeing it just now? Oh, it was beautiful alright. My entire soul held the urge to walk straight into it. That would, of course, be absurd, but I couldn't tear away from it. That was until something struck me like a dog bite from behind me.

"Thinking about something, Paul?" Chess whispered in my ear after she grabbed my arm and dangled me over my potential death. My chest wasn't quite yet over the opening, but if she let go, I wouldn't just fall. I would plunge.

"Wait, wait, wait," There was no faking it, I looked utterly pathetic. "We can elaborate on this. Can't we?" Sometimes I didn't know how to persuade Chess to do anything, but if this was just a counterfeit, illegitimate version of her, I thought begging might work out somehow.

"What's wrong?" Ren asked. "Is this the moment where you ponder over your failures and wish the one that got away hadn't?"

"I don't think this is the appropriate time or place to be doing that, mate. I have a few nutters after me right now."

"Aww." Chess magically appeared on the other side of me, holding my other arm now. "That's the nicest thing you've ever said about me." Actually, she might not have been wrong about that.

"Look! Just tell me what you need me to do, and I'll do it." My patchy throat wasn't going to hold up for much longer.

"Paul," Chess eased into a different movie villain. Now she held a crazed motherly stance. Worried about never seeing her child again. "Remember the time I helped you out of that club? What was it called again?"

I knew exactly what she was talking about, and though I didn't wanna give her the satisfaction, the words couldn't help themselves.

"Hotz N' Chill," I responded through gritted teeth.

"Stupid name for a club, right?" Right.

"What's your point?"

She grasped my arm, only this time tighter. "Do you remember what happened after I told you we'd been compromised and you couldn't go through with the faux check? I pulled you aside. Literally. What happened after I fell and people were chasing us?"

I still remembered the look on her face when that happened. "I left you behind."

Once again, her grasp tightened as she subtly laughed into my face. "No. Sweetheart. No. You looked deep into my eyes, saw I needed help, and *then* you left me behind. Thank God it wasn't Ren, though. He would be dead in a ditch somewhere."

"Exactly! You got out, didn't you?" This was the wrong response. The *really* wrong response.

"Oh my God. Both of you need to learn how to interact with humans. Pretty damn pathetic. You sound worse than Ren." The only person that treated Ren worse than me was Chess. Sometimes I felt guilty seeing his reaction to our treatment. This was not one of those times.

When Chess finally let me go, it wasn't a dramatic separation of the touching skin. It was that same, tender look.

"Why can't you just tell me what to do so I can get out of here?" There it was again. That desperation shaking in my voice.

"You know that's not how it works. Yes, it's a test, but there are some people who want you to pass, and then there are...the others."

This. This was the second biggest clue we had besides the copper. What was this hidden war? And what were they battling about?

"Fine," I whispered, having no plan as to what I was about to do next. All I could do was look past the cliff imagining what it would be like to not just be free on the other side, but to be alone on the other side. Just a single moment of solidarity with no one asking anything of me. No expectations. Not a thing to think about. A place where every muscle in my body could simply stay calm for a little while.

Just the thought of that gave me peace of mind and just a touch of hope. Until something erased me from the trance; a loud, distant scream.

"FAAAA," was all I understood, but I knew it was aimed towards me. No one else was here? Well, no one else *real* was here. Who else would they be screaming at?

"Do you hear that?" I asked, yet no one was there. Chess and Ren had vanished. Out of nowhere. No sound of footsteps, or the wind brushing against their jackets as they turned to leave. Hopefully their sudden absences were a good sign.

"FAAAAAAA!" The screams lasted longer and longer until I finally heard the full word. *"FAAAAAALL!"*

FALL! It was Chess, and she wanted me to...oh no.

All of a sudden, the valley looked much deeper and darker. How could this be the clue? And where the hell was she screaming from?

I couldn't help but scurry back, away from the edge, hoping there would be a different answer. Could something else fall from the cliff? Then again, there was no cave at the moment. How was I to get to the next level? I could only hope that meant we were nearing the end.

"I'm sorry," I said to no one, but that was it. Nothing else needed to be said. All of a sudden, sentimentality rushed through me just in case I was making the stupidest mistake of my life. "I'm - I'm just sorry." Who knew who I was even apologizing to? But it felt generic and appropriate enough for possible last words.

Welp, as Chess would say. *Here we go.*

I always knew Chess was a reckless driver, but after she hit her fifth mailbox it brought her negligence to a whole new level. I wasn't sure if the fact that she was doing this just to make me uneasy made it better or worse. Did it matter though? This wasn't the real Chess anyway.

"Where are we headed now?" I asked, feeling like I was about to pass out.

"Shhh," Chess hushed, putting her finger to her lips and looking at me in the mirror. "It's a surprise. Don't spoil the surprise."

Chess, of all people, knew I hated surprises. There was nothing logical about them. Why would I not want to know what was about to happen to me? I usually liked knowing when people were about to scream in my face and jump out from behind the couch.

But Chess? Chess mellowed in my reactions. There were multiple incidents of her telling me she took my phone and texted my ex, saying we should "get together." Damn, I should have never given her my passcode.

An idea slowly sank into me as I sulked down memory lane.

"Hey," I said. "I'm not feeling too well. Can we pull over?"

"Sure," Chess responded to my surprise. Something about her response was off. Her smile was too crisp. Like she was expecting me to say that. But no matter. Something needed to steer her off course.

"What's up, Ren?" Paul asked, watching me get out of my car.

"I just feel like I'm about to vomit." I was fine, but it was a snap reaction. For some reason, I needed to say that and I didn't know why. I was someone's voodoo doll.

"Poor, Ren," Chess whined.

"I'll be okay. I just need a break. I get car sick really easily." No. What I needed was time to think. Alone. Chess and Paul didn't seem to mind that I stumbled behind the car where they couldn't see me. "Oh, no." There was no way I could fake vomiting. They wouldn't hear anything come out, but faking other bodily noises would be substantial.

"Ooff," Paul mumbled after I blew a raspberry into my elbow. "You good, mate?"

"I'm fine. Just give me a few more minutes." They probably stopped buying it after the next three or four times, but I didn't have a plan yet. Would escaping be the logical goal? The two maniacs on the other side of my van could have held me against my will at any moment. Contemplation was nothing but a waste of time. Whatever decision was to be made, I needed to make it now.

"Maybe it was that burger you ate?" Paul didn't do well with hiding his laughter.

The last thing that I wanted to do was put in the effort to come up with a snarky remark in return, but I didn't need to. The second that my eyes laid on the keys still stabbing into the ignition, I found my way out.

"Nah, maybe there was just something in that cave that...I was allergic to?" I couldn't even comprehend what I was saying, let alone those two. But it didn't matter. Before I knew it, my arms threw open the door, twisted the old key, and off I went with a good slam into the gas pedal.

"WHAT?!" Paul screamed. I didn't bother to look in the rearview mirror to see if they were following me. They wouldn't catch up, and Chess hated taking taxis. Still, I could feel their anger. Rare was the day that I outsmarted them. Not that I ever needed to, but whenever a puzzle needed to be solved that didn't involve my technological skills, Chess or Paul were the first ones to dissect the situation. Usually, I would be on the side lines, listening in and putting in low effort to remind myself I wasn't completely worthless.

"Shit," I whispered to myself. Cursing wasn't usually my style, but I found it to be appropriate for this situation. Nothing seemed normal. My head, my heart rate, my eyes all blurred into one, unable to control what was about to happen next.

After replaying what just happened over and over in my head, I realized two things; I didn't know where I was going, and the wheels on Vanessa were turning way too fast. This was

Atlanta. There were always people on the road. And they. Went. Fast. I might as well have called up my insurance company and apologized ahead of time.

The engine calmed down, but I still couldn't. What was wrong with those two? More importantly, why wasn't I more afraid? The unearthed smiles they gave me, the unflattering tones that they never used. Nothing added up, but I didn't have enough of the equation to give an answer. Neither of them were going to give it to me either. Staying with them would be useless.

Damn, I thought. Why was I thinking this? These were my colleagues. People that, for some reason, I trusted. What if they were right? Maybe staying in this city was nothing but destructive. I mean, look at what happened to us. Even if we did leave and go our separate ways, we could be on the run for the rest of our lives.

The next few minutes were more like a few hours. Nothing changed, and everything dragged on. My chills, my drowsiness, my lack of food. *Oh shit,* FOOD! Why didn't I notice all of the places I passed? Or...did I? It didn't matter now. The next fast food restaurant that graced my presence would be the winner, and it would stay the winner for the rest of my life. The person handing me my food in a greasy brown bag would get a juicy, wet kiss. That is if they said it was okay, of course.

Wendy's appeared on my right almost immediately. Odd. I was actually thinking about how much I craved Wendy's. I suppose it was fate.

The smell of fried chicken pounded into my nose harsher than it usually did. Not that this was a bad thing by any means. In a way that meant I was going to enjoy the meal even more.

"Hello," said the oddly sly voice over the microphone. "What can I get for you?" It didn't bother me that they left out the words, "Welcome to Wendy's"...yet.

"Hi, can I get three chicken sandwiches with cheese and four large frosties?" My stomach ordered that. Not me. I swear.

"Coming right up." No announcement of the price. No clarifying which window to go to, but why should I care about that? These poor, underpaid workers only needed to give me my diabetes in a bag. They could say whatever they wanted. They were still getting a big sloppy kiss. Again, only if they said it was okay.

The wait wasn't bad considering all of the cars that ordered before me disappeared. Not to worry. I was certain they were in a hurry and rushed out of there to eat their food. I understood the rush.

Now was the time for some music. Good music. Vanessa still had a CD player within her, so I popped in my favorite Bollywood soundtrack and danced along, ready for the best meal of my life.

Bong, bong, bong, ding, ding, ding!

I almost forgot how much I missed music along with everything else. It was how we connected with our soul after all.

The music continued to play after I pulled up to the window, and I, of course, continued to jam. But all good things must come to an end. Especially when your stalker is about to serve you food.

"CHESS?" I screeched after my unexpected shock at seeing her with a headset and Wendy's uniform.

"What's the matter, sweetheart?" It wasn't the crooked smile that got to me. It was the eyes that popped out of her head and barely hid lids to cover them.

"AHHHH!" My scream was probably louder than the skidding tires that squeaked as I, once again, stabbed my foot into the gas pedal so violently I almost broke it. But the most disappointing and disturbing part? I forgot my food.

What the fuck was that?

This wasn't real life. This wasn't a dream either. Of course. It was a hallucination. Side effects of being trapped in an endless cave for so long. Damn it. How long was this going to last? Was I even able to eat now without seeing Chess's wide-eyed face? That sounded like a messed-up kink that people have.

Okay, okay, calm down. I had to repeat this over and over again in my head before I actually did. *Just try again. Next food place.* But did I even need food if this was a hallucination? Or was only half of this experience a hallucination?

I had to try again anyway, right? Maybe it was just my deprivation of food. Yes. That had to be it. Onto Pizza Palace...or whatever it was called.

My aching stomach had the wonderful idea of making me blank out for a few seconds before I saw the name, "PIZZA PALACE" on a sign, leading to a big pizza restaurant. Funny. I was sure I just made that name up, but pizza clouded my mind too much to ponder it any longer.

"Yeah, baby!" I hollered before the blue flashing lights came on behind me. "Really?" I didn't get pulled over often, but when I did, the struggle of acting like a normal human being pushed straight into me like a bullet. It would have been nice to have the real Chess here. She always happened to have really low-cut shirts when she got pulled over.

Damn it, I thought as I saw my hands shake again. I still needed food, but why was I such a wimp? Could anything really scare me after what I just went through?

"License and registration," said the deep, familiar voice leaning to the window.

"Yes, Officer. I just - WHOA!" It was no officer. Over my shoulder stood the asshole impersonating Paul in my brain.

"Is something the matter?" This encounter rang differently than the short one I just had with Chess. Paul wasn't smiling. Contrary to what many people think, Paul usually smiles. He had nice, white teeth for a British person. That only made his resting bitch face all the more terrifying.

"No, no, Officer. Nothing's the matter." I didn't know why I was still calling him "Officer." Actually, forget that. I knew exactly why. I still didn't understand what was happening. Which parts of this were real and which were fake? At the moment I was leaning towards the probability that most of my visuals and audio were fake but manually altered by someone.

"Are you sure?" He tilted his thin, Paris Hilton sunglasses to look me straight in the eye with the same blank expression on his face.

"Positive. I'm sorry, Officer, but I need to go." The license and registration were still in his hand, and the lights were still on. This time I didn't completely demolish the gas pedal. Just a little, but that was only because Paul was a relatively large man and hitting him could cause all types of commotion that I didn't want to learn more about.

Holy shit, holy shit, holy shit. How do I get out of this?

It sounded like I was going to stay put in my mom van for quite some time. For now, that was the only answer I could come up with; *Just keep driving.*

It wasn't until a few minutes later that I even had room in my brain to realize no one was following me. So, I was right. At least most of this wasn't real. Chess and Paul weren't real. The only thing in this environment that had to be authentic was me. Otherwise I wouldn't be so goddamn hungry. But food would have to wait. Just as long as I was still alive, it was now the last priority.

The roads became suspiciously curvier. I wasn't familiar with this part of Atlanta. Many backroads that caused my stomach to tip sideways mapped out the land, but I wasn't the conductor. Just like everything else happening in this place, someone else was turning my wheels the way they wanted them to be turned. Who knew where this person was taking me. Although, what was I to do but let them? That's how this worked, right?

Naturally, my head started bopping to the music that I didn't even recognize before I realized I had never turned the radio on. I must have been the only person in the world that still used the radio.

"Mhm....hmm," Someone mumbled over the static-filled station before it cleared up. "Tonight, we give you breaking news of a man that just ran away from the police. The suspect has been identified as Ren Patel."

They were joking, right? Literally joking. "THEY DIDN'T EVEN COME AFTER ME!" They didn't even bother to announce what I did wrong. Which, from what these imposters knew, was nothing. Somehow it took me a second to notice it was Paul speaking over the radio, but no confusion or anger disturbed me anymore. I wouldn't let it.

"The suspect is known to be dangerous and -" But the static interrupted Paul's voice with a screaming one. It took me a moment to register, but I almost jumped out of my seat for the hundredth time that night.

"FAAAAAALL!" This had to be a joke, but it was the only part of this hallucination I had a true connection to. The clarity, the voice, it called to me. *"FAAAAAALL!"* Chess

repeated the same word over and over again. Wait...how did I know it was Chess?

Idiot. Of course, it was Chess. This was the clue. It had to be, and she was screaming it to us to save us. The only thing was, what did that mean? Fall from what? But I didn't need to know. Vanessa would figure it out.

"Alright, girl," I said, rubbing the wheel. "Bring me to them."

Like I said before, Paul and Chess could resolve a situation in no time. I didn't have to worry about Paul deciphering Chess's clue. We would all be back in the tunnel in no time. Shit.

Vanessa drove faster and faster without my having to step on the gas pedal. We were getting closer to wherever we needed to be. I could feel it. Suddenly in the distance, the ocean's horizon beamed in the navy-blue sky, and Vanessa refused to stop or turn before the pier. It didn't hit me. Instead, the realization of what needed to happen sank into me with only a touch of fear. Nothing I couldn't handle. We needed to drive off the dock and into the ocean.

"Good thing this isn't real life."

I was ready. If someone wanted to actually kill me, they would have done it by now. They would have done it a *looong* time ago. Nothing was going to happen to me. I would wake up again.

Vanessa continued to increase speed. She was having a blast. Three hundred feet. Two hundred now...

"And here. We. GOOOOOO!"

23:
CHESS

The bleeding mainly stopped, but any liveliness I had still dragged out of me. With the little eye sight that I had, I noticed the scab already getting darker. This wasn't gonna be a battle wound to be proud of. Maybe a tattoo over it would look cool. Man, that would have to be one giant ass tattoo.

I hadn't even had the chance to notice that Fake Ren and Fake Paul were gone, but I was still trapped. The handcuffs were going nowhere anytime soon. Guess this was just another piece of the puzzle. A giant, pointy, obnoxious piece.

Keys, keys, keys.

Maybe the wannabe Men in Black messed up and took the keys with them. Or maybe they just wanted to see me in pain while I struggled to pull my hand out of the cuff. The second option sounded much more realistic...in this scenario at least.

"Kill me now," I pleaded sincerely while I scrunched my right hand as far as it would go. "Ahhhhh!" My volume crescendoed as a result of my thumb almost popping out of its socket. The edge of the metal cut so deeply into my skin, it almost immediately started dripping blood. Great. That was certainly what I needed more of.

This couldn't possibly work, my asshole subconscious kept saying to me over and over again. It didn't help that I needed to take breaks in order to endure the pain. Thank the Lord I never had kids, and was never gonna. Breaks were probably not an option during the crowning portion of birth.

The room fell completely silent after I settled my mind. The pain, my surroundings, the imposters. It was all in my head. Every little bit was a trick.

"AHHHHH!" I screamed without counting down. That would have only freaked me out more, but with a little pop and a big crunch, my hand fully slipped out of the cuff.

There was no rush to continue to whatever the next step would be. Never in my life have I endured that much pain. My foggy brain and fatigued limbs wouldn't let me do anything but lay uncomfortably on the wood with my one bleeding, free hand over my stomach. I was so scared to look at it. How could there be any guarantee of still owning a thumb after that? Maybe I just dislocated it.

My breath and heartbeat refused to slow down, even after I gave them a shit ton of time. I figured losing this much blood would have temporarily damaged my heart, but apparently someone refused to let me stop. I should have figured.

The other thing that needed calming more than anything was my mind. If only it was able to pull me into a world where I knew what time it was, or what was on the T.V. tonight. I wanted to worry about first-world problems again so badly.

Reminiscing wasn't exactly the word I would use to describe my procrastination. Reflection would be more like it. I craved some sort of a smile. Not peace of mind, not happiness, just something that could bring me a slice of normalcy. Normal was comfortable. Something I understood and knew how to deal with. I was probably the only nurse in the world that couldn't stand the sight of my own blood. That's right. Other people's blood was never a bother. My own blood? If I wasn't already lying down, I probably would have hit my head on the floor from the dizziness. This wasn't normal. The panic and repulsion weren't part of the order of things. The longer I waited for the shock to disintegrate, the better.

"Okay," I whispered to myself and whoever was listening. "I'm okay. Whatever happens I'll live. I can fight through this." My voice faded into a deeper tremble and deflation. I didn't fully believe what I was saying, but it was nice to hear. Especially from me, of course.

The courage finally broke into me before I looked down to see my dislocated thumb. I'd seen worse, but I couldn't watch as I somehow immediately snapped it back in. I guess the fear overpowered the disgust and pain.

"Ahhhh!" I screamed after hearing the repulsive popping sound. How did I never know that popping a joint back in hurts worse than popping it out? Damn it, I never should have been a nurse.

Now, the only problem was freeing the other hand, because I was sure as hell not doing that again. I'd rather saw my other arm off. That's right. *Arm*. Not just the hand. Full arm.

The keys were nowhere to be found, but the place was messy enough that paper clips and pencils weren't that hard to find. The only trouble was the fact that none of them stood close to me. This was gonna take some time.

From my trapped placement, it was difficult to see what the hell I was laying on, but it seemed like simple plywood that was somehow screwed into the floor. Now, this shit wasn't light by any means, but not moving it didn't seem like much of an option. Besides these thunder thighs weren't made for nothing.

"Come on," I told my...well I wasn't sure which part of me I was talking to. Any movement would do, but not a single part of my body needed any more motivation when I spotted a rusty, two-inch nail about six feet to my left. "Jesus, thank you." That was the first time I ever uttered those words.

It didn't seem that far away. Maybe it was reachable, but it would be a stretch. A long, discomforting stretch that would test my flexibility to the max. My aching shoulder almost dislocated as I pulled away from the wooden board and still couldn't reach the stupid nail. It was too risky anyway putting myself in that amount of pain again. No matter how familiar I was with putting a shoulder back in place, I was not in the mood to deal with that shit again.

If I couldn't reach the nail with my foot, I was gonna have to dislocate another thumb. Luckily my Doc Martens made my legs an inch and a half longer. It wasn't until I reached my right foot out that I realized how weak my core was. Maybe it was just the hunger, but I couldn't hold myself up and extend my body far enough. Only one sucky option was left. I would have to use my arm with the shitty thumb to hold myself up.

"This better work," I told myself, already regretting making the right and only decision. "Ahhhh!" I tried to suppress my outburst. Not that it mattered at all. There was no one here to be brave for, but I was only about fifty percent successful anyway. The pain distracted me to the point where I almost forgot why I was destroying the nerves in my arm any further, but my foot kicked the nail straight to my reach before I could pass out from the pain.

The nail fumbled around in my broken hand, but all of the images and noises jumbled around in my head. The eagerness shook from my skin. I couldn't focus, but I didn't need to. It all happened so quickly. One second, I was popping the other handcuff off my wrist, and the next I was bursting out of the room. Nothing in between. I *ran.*

Finding my way out wasn't hard. Only one opening stood in the wall, with a high archway and no door. A staircase immediately appeared to my right, which I would normally roll my eyes at because I hate taking the stairs, but the energy I was able to muster pulled me up before I could feel any negative impact. After tripping up the stairs only twice, I noticed the most beautiful sight; light. Light fell like a feather onto the brown stones that made up the stairs. I was getting close to the outside. But I didn't have time to stop and admire my accomplishment. Not because of my antsy jitters, but because before I knew it, I was standing under an archway that led straight to the smooth, green grass.

Fall, fall, fall, I repeated to myself. What was there to fall from? All that surrounded me were trees, rocks, and dirt. *Trees.* That was too easy. Well, maybe not too easy, per se, but it wasn't fitting. It wouldn't have the same sort of flare as the other solutions. I had to keep looking. I had to keep running. My mind kept pulling me away from what I needed to be looking for. Instead the shock of my continuing energy lingered in the back of my head. How was I doing this? I didn't have any food or water in my stomach. I barely slept the previous four or so days, and adrenaline only goes so long. Who was it that was trying to kill us, but also assist in our tragic journey at the same time? And how on Earth were they injecting artificial energy into me?

After maybe a mile of running, I managed to refocus my mind on the next step in the mission. Maybe it needed to be some sort of dramatic retelling of *Alice in Wonderland.* Was there a rabbit hole anywhere? Or something big that I could jump into? That would fit the theme perfectly. A dark hole where you can't see the bottom and you feel like you're stoned as all hell. My eyes pressed against the ground, searching and searching without giving it another thought, but another thought was for sure needed, which I realized the second I ran up to what looked like the literal end of the world. I knew exactly why it was there...and I knew it immediately.

"You've got to be fucking kidding me." Even my soft voice echoed into the endless void that was the sky. To be fair, it still stuck with the theme. The dark brown dirt refused to let me

136

see the bottom, and I was definitely gonna feel something falling down this thing.

If I made it, I would survive, right? That would just be stupid, but what if I didn't jump far enough and I hit my head on the edge? What if I had a heart attack before I landed? But for the millionth time during this entrapment, I needed to remind myself that I had no other choice.

"Chess, babe, you can do this. It'll be fun." I didn't believe that last part for a second until I dove like I used to as a child into a swimming pool. Middle finger leading. Toes pointed. I was falling, dripping, sinking down into whatever universe I was ripping into.

The wind almost pulled out my hair, until I came to an abrupt, but not painful stop. Even animators from Pixar probably wouldn't be able to recreate this scene. My limbs, skin, and hair all floated in slow motion as if inertia was never a law of motion. But the best part? My nose and toes hovered five inches above what almost looked like an old kitchen floor, but I didn't have time to dissect every detail. From the time my ghost-like flying stopped to when my entire body smacked against the floor in the snap of a finger, I might have been able to fit in a single tequila shot.

"Ooff!" I heard from a few feet away. For a moment, I thought it was just my echo, but when my dumbass brain realized there were two other voices and both were way too low to be mine, I dragged my bloody nose off the floor to see Ren and Paul in the exact same position that I was.

"Is everyone okay?" Paul asked, or at least I thought that's what he said. His face was still muffled into the ground, answering his own question.

"When I figure out if we're alive or not, I'll let you know," Chess replied.

For our age, it took us way too long to stand up and even longer to know we weren't back in the tunnel.

"What?" I mumbled. Wherever we were, it looked like a witch's lair in a children's story book, but much bigger and much fancier. Maybe a tower or giant well due to the cylindrical shape of the room. Everything was in tip-top shape. The wooden couches and chairs were smooth and styled. Nothing was chipped or showed any signs of wear and tear. Someone had a lot of time on their hands.

"Where are we?" Chess asked, but before anyone could find an answer, I felt a pair of strong arms shove me back to the floor.

"What the - ?" It didn't take me long to realize what he was doing.

"What's my middle name?" He asked. Really? He chose that question to make sure we were real?

"Paul, I -"

"WHAT IS IT? YOU HAVE A LAUGH AT IT ALL THE TIME!"

"IT'S EUGENE!"

"Paul, knock it off," Chess calmly, yet intensely spoke.

"Don't." Paul snapped his arm and focus to her. "You're next."

"Paul." Chess puffed out her chest to heighten her sense of superiority. "You can ask us as many questions as you want. Those things knew too much about us."

Paul carried on breathing heavily in my face, but after a few moments of silence. Paul backed away without admitting that she was right.

The next few minutes, or in all honesty it could have been days, were suddenly a blur. Not a mystery, just a colorful blur.

"Damn," I whispered to myself while my brain juggled with my current surroundings and previous ones. "I think I was in a car." Slowly it came back to me. "Yeah, yeah, yeah. I was in a car and I drove...wow...I drove off a dock and into the ocean."

"I don't have the energy to be shocked right now," said Chess. She had a point considering I was still a bit wet. She couldn't tear her eyes away from the room. The energy horrified me, but she was entranced. Something also told me that her last location was a bit hazy too.

This little fairy house would have sold instantly on a tiny home website. Whoever designed this had style, but old style. Tales told in a modern fashion had a different and unique mood to them. Modern elements weren't portrayed in old tales, just like the essence of this room. Whoever lived here had been here for a while, and probably never left.

"Don't touch anything," said Chess, coming close to touching every inch of this place herself. I didn't blame her. Not only was the presentation and flare of the room exquisite, but there wasn't a spec of dirt to be found. Not even on the stone walls. Not on the antique chairs that sat in a circle on the upper platform in the circular room. Don't get me wrong, it was dark as all hell. Especially since there was no ceiling, just endless darkness, but the finished polish would squeak if you ran your finger across it. However, I only knew that because Paul felt so inclined to do so.

"Paul!" I loudly whispered.

"What did I say?" Chess also loudly whispered, thinking she was the boss.

"Why are we whispering all of a sudden?" Paul asked, mocking us.

"We don't know who's here!" Chess lost her patience. Up until now, she had hidden her fear fairly well. Abrupt collisions never truly bothered her or threw her off course, but after whatever happened to her purple hand, something probably changed.

"If someone was going to show up, where are they?" I asked with a bad feeling in my stomach.

"Maybe we have to do something first," Paul suggested.

"Another fucking clue?" Chess asked.

"No." I still wasn't sure why I shut that idea down, but it just didn't seem right. For the past few days there were countless instances where we just knew what to do next. Like someone was slapping the ideas into our heads. Why would this be any different?

"Let's just continue to look around," said Paul, already doing so.

The place wasn't filled with many knick knacks, but what we found supported my theory. Countless dolls lined up on the circular wall, but no Barbies. Degas paintings stacked on top of each other, but no posters of One Direction (or whoever was popular these days).

"Hey look at this." Chess pointed out a television that sat right in the center of the room, but stood the size of an iPad mini. No wonder we didn't see it until now. Besides, the number of fluffy stuffed animals piled on top of it caught our attention instead.

"Everything else here looks like it's from the eighteen or nineteen hundreds," said Paul. "Why is there an old telly?"

"Guess somebody wanted an upgrade." Chess was too invested in the old television to give a straight answer. Carefully, she used the little light we had to find a piece of paper hidden under the miniature television.

"Turn me on," Chess read after unfolding the paper. "Clearly this girl is too innocent for modern society."

"How do you know it's a girl?" I asked.

"We all agreed the whispers were from a woman, right?" We nodded in agreement. "Besides, gender norms were regimented a bit more back then." She gestured to the dolls and stuffed animals.

It only took a few seconds for Chess to realize the "on" button wasn't a button at all, and she had to turn the knob in order to turn it on, but the screen didn't display the news or the latest baseball game. Instead, a young woman, no older than twenty, plastered her face on the screen, from the waist up. The television gave no color, but with what I could see, her hair was blonde with tight ringlets, and her rosy cheeks beamed bright with her wide smile. Her short sleeve blouse might have been pink, (it also might have been a dress) but she began reciting her somewhat robotic speech before I could investigate further.

"Hello," she projected. I could already tell how delicate and high pitched her voice was. "By now you may have countless questions."

"Is she serious?" I asked.

"Shhhh," Chess mumbled, putting her hand in my face without looking at me.

"I hope I can answer some of those questions for you," the girl continued. "I'm sure I'll have many questions for you too. For instance, was my tiger nice to you? Or did my bees sting you? If so, did it hurt? I sure hope they maintained their manners. I deeply apologize for not carrying a full first aid kit." The more she went on, the more I realized how much I would rather be locked in a room with the Annabelle doll over this girl. "But let's not get into that yet. We still have a few more things to discuss.

"First of all, let me formally introduce myself. My name is Patience. Patience Manning. I am nineteen years old, and have been nineteen years old since the year 1803." I could see the light turn on above Paul's head, then explode. We figured this girl had been down here for a while, but 1803? "I've been trapped down here since my nineteenth birthday. All thanks to my father, but blaming him won't be necessary. First of all, he's dead. Second, after the first few decades of living here I finally reached the conclusion that he was merely trying to protect me. And don't worry. I know your curiosity must be eating at you right now. I'll tell you everything."

I didn't think it was possible for someone's high-pitched laugh to sound so ghoulish, but the intensity of her voice when vibrating with a serious tone made up for it. She cleared her throat like the Queen of England before she continued. "As I said, my nineteenth birthday came around, and Father got nervous. I already had told him I was ready to leave and go to college the year before on my eighteenth birthday, but he made it quite clear that was only acceptable for boys to do. A woman's place was with the children at home, and my time was running out to find a potential suitor.

"Well, towards the end of the day, I told Father exactly what I wanted and how I was going to get it. I didn't think I wanted children, and I was determined to make money on my own. He responded by telling me he had already found a match for me. I was furious, but he never liked it when I got angry with him. He made that clear whenever he would beat me with that tiger statue, or try and smother me with my pillow. Sometimes he would even threaten to beat me with one of the rocks from the garden. Thank goodness he never did. He would only ever do that with Lyle. Anyway, I kept my mouth shut, but a few hours later this man met us for dinner in our home. He was fine, I suppose, but Father, well let's just say he was getting a little too eager. He thought this was supposed to be the best birthday present of all."

Her chin didn't fall, but her eyes dropped to the floor, and her mouth tensed as she tried to release the words. The discomfort surrounded the room, encompassing all four of us, but something told me the three of us felt at least a hint of sympathy for this girl.

"He wouldn't stop yelling at me!" Her voice raised. "I was an awfully quiet child. I simply didn't think I had much to say, but Father was begging me to instantly fall in love with him, so somebody could take care of me. Perhaps he was just tired of doing it himself, or maybe he preferred worrying about my younger brother, Lyle. Either way, the night was coming to an end, and when this man finally decided to propose, I didn't refuse, but I did say that I would need to think about it first. I must say, I thought I'd seen all of the anger a man could produce, but that night, I witnessed anger mixed with offense."

It was like watching a movie, knowing an innocent person was sitting with the killer in the car. The suspense disturbed us all, but there was nothing we could do. "What was I supposed to do? Father never even tortured me in such a way. Then again, Father did nothing when this man tried to drown me in the stream behind the house. Nevertheless, it was all over rather quickly. If Lyle's baseball bat hadn't been right next to me when he finally let me back in the house, I probably wouldn't be here today. I probably also wouldn't have had to clean up so much blood on that kitchen table.

"Anyway, we buried this man's body in the backyard, but that wasn't the end of it. You see, my father's sister tried to cover up her sins by pretending to be the local apothecary owner. In reality, she was the local alchemist. In my opinion, she wasn't the most talented of her craft, but oh, the things that she could get away with. In other words, she was the one that created this tunnel.

"It didn't take her very long. Most of the creatures, supplies, she already had all of that in storage. But I didn't pay much attention to what she was doing. I was too busy being pinned down by my brother and father. They were so scared. Especially Father. Back then, the world wasn't what it is today. Young girls faced no mercy when taking somebody that was loved away. Besides, when young women, such as myself, showed any sort of strength, men feared for the disappearance of their control. That's what I learned being raised in a house with no women other than myself. Honestly, I never even asked what happened to my mother. That was until my father told me she was stung by multiple bees that made her heart stop.

"Anyway, Father's main goal was to see if any potential suitors would be strong enough for me. That was his idea, anyway, when he trapped me in here. Eventually, it wasn't working. I needed more than two people at a time, and they had to be smart. Not physically strong, smart. I began luring anyone down here. Anyone who I, and my nephew, thought suitable. I simply needed to leave. I gave up on the marriage idea a long time ago. That was never going to get me out of this tunnel. This cave was becoming a part of me, and I won't lie to you, it was overwhelming. I'm still not sure how, but the spirits within this place started to obey me in a way. They trusted me. Eventually, I was even able to use my voice to give clues to whomever deserved them. The magic grew stronger every year, but it still took work to relieve me from this place. Part of me believed Father never meant for that to happen anyway.

"You might be wondering why I'm telling you all of this. The truth is, I haven't had many other people to talk to. If you're watching this, it means you have proceeded further than anyone else has. The rest are dead, in case you were wondering. So sorry to say, but congratulations. You're also probably wondering why you need to be down here, in my chambers, in the first place. Well, those answers are one in the same really, but I can't tell you just yet. For I have one more clue to give you."

"You've got to be kidding me," Chess whispered.

"Shhhh," Paul and I both mocked her.

"I think you're going to like this one," Patience continued. The room fell so silent, one could hear a pin drop, and the ringing would sting your ears. The anticipation was killing us before she finally said, with such precise annunciation, "Leave."

"Leave?" We all repeated.

"That's right, leave." She knew we would be questioning her judgment. "You didn't think I was going to keep you here, did you? I'm sure by now you know that it's not that simple, but think it over. I'm sure at least one of you will figure it out. Just give me a moment to freshen up, and I'll be right in. Enjoy!"

She twiddled her fingers before Chess threw her hands over her head and said, "Really? No. No. No." Her panic didn't help Paul and me one bit.

"Oh, and one more thing," said Patience before turning off the camera. "In case you were wondering if I've been watching you this whole time including now, you'd be right. Don't disappoint me."

25:
PAUL

All six of our feet took over. Pacing was the only thing that made all of us look like we were trying to contemplate what Patience could have meant by her clue. She probably was already disappointed in us, but after over two hundred years, I think she could wait a few more hours.

"Is there a bathroom in this place?" Chess asked. I couldn't believe I was thinking this, but how the hell did she have anything to pass through her bladder? "Is there even food in here? Does this person eat?"

"Why are you thinking about this right now?" Ren asked with a clenched jaw.

"Because I can, and contrary to popular belief, food usually does help people think."

"No. That's when people actually *have* food."

I couldn't take it anymore. "Oh, would you just shut it?" I didn't have the energy to use my full voice, but they got the idea. Chess had a point. Why would she be thinking at all when what she needed more than anything was fuel? I couldn't blame her, but Ren looked more distraught than all of us, but in a strange way, and I couldn't figure out why. But the last thing that I wanted to do was ask him. For the first time, I felt hesitant to inspire the snapping of his voice and temper.

"Has anyone checked to see if there are any open doors?" Chess asked after a few moments of silence. The thought had occurred to me a few times, but that was too easy. The only opening I saw was a metal, bolted trapped door behind the sofa on the lower level.

"Only that over there," I said, pointing to it. Chess gathered up enough energy to bolt over to the trapped door and try to yank it open, but the metal didn't even jiggle. Her refusal to give up gave me the impression she didn't appreciate that one bit.

"It won't open," she said, finally standing back up and leaving it alone.

"Really?" I sarcastically asked with my hands over my cheeks. Mocking sarcasm wasn't my usual approach to Chess's impatience, but for now, her reaction was worth it.

"Okay, now I'm getting sick of you two." She threw herself down onto the old chair closest to her and slapped her hands together. "What do we know about this room?"

"Why does the room matter?" Ren asked, still not looking up from his lap.

"Because every clue that we've had was somehow related to the objects or environment of where we were standing. So, what can we gather from this place?"

From her attitude, she was probably expecting an answer right away, but matching her energetic frustration was going to be difficult.

"Well, she said we were the first ones to get here," I started. "So, a lot of other people didn't make it."

"Right. Don't remind me," Chess snapped.

Ignoring her, I continued with, "And everything in this room looks ancient, even the telly. Although she probably got that more recently."

"So, she probably has someone still helping her, but why haven't they released her?" Chess stood up from the chair and began pacing again."

"Because they're afraid of her. Or maybe they just can't." I didn't really have to think about that. The thought just came to me.

"So, who is this person? I mean, if they're on the outside, they've been aging, but they must know who she is and what she's done."

"The same person who hired us. That Samuel guy, right? That house has probably been passed down for centuries." That wasn't too difficult to find out. Who else would it have been?

"How do we know *she* didn't hire us?" Chess, already probably forgetting Patience's name, threw her hand to the side to emphasize her annoyance.

"Maybe they both did."

"But wait. They both could have hired us, but the person who's been helping her is afraid of her, but still wants her out? How does that make any sense?"

146

"That's a good question." I didn't have an answer, but I had a better question. Why was Ren being so damn quiet? "Ren, you alive, mate?" He had grown sick of my stupid questions and remarks a while ago, but he nodded without making eye contact with me. Good enough.

"Why is she still down here? Well, we already know why. We just need to figure out why she can't get out."

This was going to be a while, and it wasn't that I was losing my patience. It was that I had already lost it, and my body was going through withdrawals. My teeth impulsively bit my nails which never happens, and my breath inhaled in a staccato pattern. Almost as if I'd been crying for hours.

"She needs people to solve the clues," said Chess. "Not her. Someone else. They have to pass all these tests."

"Yup." I tried to understand where she was going with this, but the constant repetition was more like a vinyl record spinning around again and again.

"It doesn't sound like she needs actual help with anything. It sounds like she just needs people. Like just bodies."

Something about the word *bodies* didn't sit well with me. Maybe it was just the way she said it; low and dragged. Or maybe I just watched too many serial killer documentaries. Regardless, she was leading us somewhere.

Ren still just stood there. That is, if slouching with your chin pinned to your chest with your arms crossed leaning up against the wall is what you call standing. But this time, when I noticed his lack of vocals, something hit me. What if his silence implied that he knew something. Or even better, he knew exactly what Patience's clue meant.

"Ren? Do you mind helping us?" I politely asked. There was no more time to ease him into things, even though I was well aware of his sensitivity by now.

"Why?" Ren asked, catching me off guard. "You guys seem to have it, as usual." This only confirmed my suspicions.

"No butting in and trying to impress us this time?" Chess snapped. Damn that was harsher than usual. But nonetheless Ren didn't snap back, and we stayed in silence for the next few awkward moments.

"Anywayyyy…" I re-centered my brain. We were almost there. "What else are we missing?"

"What does she mean by she just needs people to come down here and rescue her?" Chess asked. "Why can't she just escape in reverse order? And why did she say she needed more than just *two* people at a time? Wouldn't you just need *one* man at a time? Why does she need -" Suddenly Chess stood up wide-eyed and speechless, but only for a moment, per usual. "A body. She needs a body, but alive. She needs these people alive when they finally reach her. Otherwise if she just needed a body she certainly would have gotten one. She had plenty to choose from." She ignited her intense pacing. "Also, she did say that she realized having three people instead of less was more efficient. But she only needs one. Just...just one."

Her eyes turned to ice, and all of the color drained from her skin. "What?" I asked.

"She needs a replacement." Her voice never shook with such an intense vibrato. "She's gonna take one of us and keep us here. Or kill us, now that we've entered. That's probably how it works. She needs a live person to come in, and only the same amount of live people can leave!"

It was a stretch, but it all made sense. Patience probably gave us this clue, implying we were the ones who had to decide who was to leave and who was to stay in whatever state Patience deemed appropriate.

"We have to get out of here," I said as quietly as I could. This was the exact moment that our voices were going to endanger us. Patience had eyes and ears in places we didn't even know about yet. The only form of communication that was safe to use was eye contact, and even that was risky.

Chess looked around, for what I wasn't sure. That is until she spotted a large, crystal candlestick with no candle in it. The only weapon available in this room. Ren could have passed out for all we knew. He apparently wanted nothing to do with needing to get out of here. It didn't matter. As usual Chess and I had it covered. I nodded to her, confirming I comprehended what she was trying to communicate. The plan was shitty as all hell, but it was something. Frantically, I looked around, hoping for another plan. Not necessarily another weapon, but any other option as an alternative or in addition to the candlestick. Just for some reassurance, but something in my soul and mind went blank and white. It wasn't the lack of focus or the anxiety that filled the room from all three of us. It was the presence of another human being entering the room. If you could call a sparkling essence floating from thin air into the form of a person a human being.

"Good idea," Patience whispered from behind Chess and into her ear. Chess barely even flinched. Her tension wouldn't allow any more surprises. "My dears, have we decided?"

26:
CHESS

It wasn't my ear that received the whisper, but it nearly made me pass out. Suddenly I felt too claustrophobic to move. The darkness pulled into the four of us, highlighting nothing but our faces. Patience stood loosely, but with more energy than the rest of us. She smiled at us as if she was now a part of a new friend group.

"So, what have we decided?" Patience asked, once again, with intertwined fingers under her chin. We were all still too flabbergasted to answer. This was by far the most intricate, supernatural, and also intrusive thing we'd seen on this journey. And this teenager presented it as so...normal. "Oh, please. I knew you must have guessed it when you stopped talking to each other. It's really hard to keep secrets from me in this place, you know."

"And -" Paul muttered. The words barely escaped his mouth. "What is this place exactly?"

"I apologize. Did I not make that clear?" Instead of answering orally, we just barely shook our heads. "We're underground, silly. Was that not obvious? Many things in this tunnel aren't what they seem. Amusing isn't it? But some things are exactly what they seem. You're only overthinking it. By the way, well done. Samuel is my nephew, and yes he did hire you upon my request."

"Right," I said, barely articulating. Her speech delayed in my brain for a few seconds. Mainly because her soft voice was giving me PTSD from hearing her whispers in my ear. It was like seeing an old boyfriend at the grocery store.

"You're hiding something from me, aren't you?" She wasn't mad. We were playing a game, and she was excited to find out what our next move was gonna be and if she was gonna win or not.

"What?" Both Ren and Paul mumbled.

"Oh seriously, gentlemen. Keep up. You're not finished yet." The three of us flinched when she took a small step forward. Lord, we were deathly afraid she was gonna touch us. "Tell me, what do you think *leave* means?" None of us said a word. It only dawned on us that killing her would be very difficult. "In all honesty, you don't have to comply with me. You can just proceed to your next engagement. I only think it'll be more fun this way."

"So, you haven't talked to anyone in the last two hundred years?" Paul asked, trying to stall.

Patience looked at him, clearly stating she was not named after the actual definition of "patience."

"Yes, I have. Well -" We all leaned in a bit closer while she pursed her lips and tilted her head to the sky. "In a way. My great-great-great-nephew is my current employee."

"Employee?" Ren asked, unappreciative of the creativity of her word use.

"Yes, employee. That's what I call them. What else would I call them?"

"I usually call them family members." Funny, Ren. But there was no room for laughter. Patience agreed.

"I've never physically met him in person, but he delivers me things that I need, or things that I simply desire."

"Like food?" Paul asked, still trying to stall.

"No, dear sir. Do you see a proper kitchen anywhere?"

Paul didn't look around before he said, "No."

"Of course you don't, and unless my eyes deceived me, I believe you saw me approaching the three of you, dissolved in the air? Do you think that kind of stomach needs food as fuel?"

"I hope not," said Ren before he could stop himself.

"With all due respect -" I began, still unsure of how to respect her. "Or if I may ask, what kind of fuel do you need?"

"I need human energy." Honestly, I was surprised she knew that, and so confidently too. I'm sure there weren't too many people around to educate her on her condition. "That's why all of the hundreds of people who have tried to pass through the tunnel weren't a complete waste. I absorbed what I could while whispering the clues in your ears. And thank you by the way for all coming down. Three people. My, I was hungry."

All of this was a complete waste of time. Any moment now she would figure out that we were trying to stall, but I couldn't see anything that would trap her...unless...

"Patience," I said. "We decided that the clue means we need to find the right way to leave. Not the easy way. So not through that trapped door."

"Mhmm." Patience smiled with no teeth. "Good eye." Something told me she was being sarcastic. It wasn't hidden very well, and we were slowly learning she was smarter than she looked.

"So, did we get it right? I mean what else is that trapped door used for?" God, I hoped and prayed she wasn't about to say it was just for storage or something stupid like that. Back in the olden days, didn't they have safe rooms, or rooms where they would lock their children away for being naughty? What if her father or nephew or whomever made a discipline room for her? Could I trap her in there?

"Let me ask you," Patience wrapped her hands behind her back like a sergeant in the military. "How did you come to this conclusion?"

"You were watching us the whole time, weren't you?" Paul asked, now losing his temper. "You tell us."

"That was rather difficult to pick up on. I also don't have seventeen eyes. I can't pick up on *everything*. So...amuse me." She wasn't buying a word of any of this.

"Honestly," said Ren. "We know each other pretty well. We all saw Chess eyeballing that trapped door earlier, and we - we couldn't think of anything else." There it was again. That tense, lethargic look from Ren. He wasn't usually this quiet, and he looked more hopeless than usual. Although, I wouldn't be surprised if he was three times as scared and shook as Paul and I were. He was always the first one to be afraid.

"Well, are we right?" I asked knowing damn straight what the answer was.

"It was an intriguing guess, but not quite." Patience kept a steady beat to her voice.

"Not quite?" Paul asked. "Were we close?"

"Think of it as more of a hole. You're missing a few key details. Details that, well let's just say, have already crossed your mind."

This woman could undoubtedly read our minds in one way or another. She'd spent over two hundred years in isolation. There's no way her people-reading skills alone were that strong no matter how many people she watched die trying to rescue her.

"There needs to be a trade," said Ren, out of nowhere. "Someone has to stay."

152

"Bloody hell, Ren," Paul loudly whispered with more anger in him than anyone else in the room. "When will you ever shut the hell up?"

"Oh!" Ren suddenly sparked an enormous energy. "So, when I'm quiet you want me to talk, and when I do talk, you want me to shut up?"

"Both of you shut the fuck up!" I snapped. "Ren, Paul is right, what's wrong with you?" I didn't want Patience to think this was a performance just for her, but I didn't want her to believe this was the truth either. I was lost. There was no clear pathway for me to follow, or for any of us to follow. For the first time, we didn't have a back-up plan.

"I hate to break up this little friendly altercation," Patience laughed, "but Ren is right. So, who will it be?"

Clearly nothing about her behavior changed in the last two hundred years. Her father probably brought her down, not to protect her, but because he was afraid of her. Who wouldn't be? "The Devil" might as well have been stamped on her forehead. Even if it wasn't, you could still see the uncontrolled anger seeping out of her eyes.

"We're not going to decide," I told her, trying not to be afraid. The second after I spoke, I hoped it wasn't one of those situations where you were picking solely because you were the first one to speak, but luckily, Patience didn't flinch.

"So," she quietly said, "does that mean I get to choose?" She was almost excited at the thought.

"No," Paul butted in. "It means that we have to figure out another way." The sympathy in his voice erupted. Guess it was time for a new approach. "We can all escape from here. I'm sure there's a way. We just have to outsmart...I suppose, your father?"

The sides of Patience's face dropped. Nobody ever spoke to her like they cared about her safety, or what she wanted. Thank God. *We were getting somewhere.*

"I don't think that's how this works," Patience responded.

"You don't *think*?" Paul asked.

Patience rolled her eyes, and to my dismay, I rolled them along with her. "You didn't know my father. There was no getting around him." She took a strong step closer to us, claiming her dominance. "So, I will ask once again, who will it be?"

The three of us exchanged looks, desperately hoping someone else had an answer, or something, *anything*. But like everything else during this encounter, we went blank.

Surprisingly, Patience didn't seem angry anymore. Her frustration faded away into thin air. Only laughter remained with her. Laughter that was a step further than unsettling. "A small part of me actually hoped it would come to this." And in the blink of an eye, she pulled a foot-long dagger out of nowhere and plunged it straight into Ren's heart.

"NOOOOO!" I screamed. But there was nothing I could do. Ren was dead before he hit the floor.

27:
PAUL

"Poor thing," Patience mocked, as she stared down at Ren's lifeless body. From the ease in her eyes, I would guess that she almost enjoyed watching the blood drip from the blade in a consistent rhythm.

"Ren?" Chess whispered for probably the fifth time. "Ren?" A single tear dropped from her cheek. It wasn't much, but I realized it was the first time that I had ever seen Chess cry. As horrible as it was to say, I never thought that this would be a reason for her to do so. "Why?" She looked up at Patience not with anger, but with utter confusion.

"Why?" Patience asked with a significant attitude. "I already divulged that information, dear."

There wasn't a fraction of a second that lingered before Chess shot straight up to standing and screamed defiantly, "NO! WHY?"

Patience needed more specificity. Her head tilted at a slight angle, and her eyes tightened briefly, but Chess's sudden bold stance gave away the real question.

"Ohhh!" Patience enlightened us with her high-pitched squeal. "You really need to ask?"

"What's that supposed to mean?" I finally broke my silence. My voice wasn't as shaky as I thought it would be.

"He was the weak one." The sudden change to distress made me jump back just a hair. Her voice now trembled with a new anger.

"How would you know that?" Chess asked, not denying it.

"How do you think I found you?" Neither of us answered. We were too busy asking ourselves why on Earth that would be an important question at the moment. That certainly wasn't what Chess had asked. "So silly. You're going to laugh."

"Laugh at what?" I asked, insisting she would stop trying to dodge our question.

"Ren was the one who brought you here. He knew everything."

I would say the room fell so silent you could hear a pin drop, but the sound of both my and Chess's heart stopping echoed throughout the room. You could also hear and even feel the tightening of our chests and lungs. What was this woman talking about?

"You're making this shit up," Chess whispered.

"Well, of course, not everything. But Chessy, I just answered your question. Isn't that what you wanted? That's how I knew what I needed to know."

"What? No." I could barely hear Chess. Her throat tightened too much, and her chest was too contracted.

"Well, maybe that was misleading. He thought that one of you two was to perish. He thought he was going to leave with endless amounts of money. Silly."

"How?" I asked. We were always with Ren. Always working, always going out. How did we not know about this? But more importantly, what did we do to him that would cause this betrayal? We weren't that horrid to him, were we?

"My nephew. He's the only relative and employee that's been truly kind to me. The only one with any variety of compassion. Don't get me wrong, every one of my sweet guardians after my father have tried to help me escape. They're the ones who have brought the people to the tunnel. Or captured. Depending on the person." The miniscule jitter in her soft laugh forced my eyes away from her. I was afraid of what would happen if I made too much eye contact with her.

"How does Ren fit into any of this?" Chess asked.

"Oh yes, well, my nephew drew up a new scheme. What if we found a few people and did a little research on them prior to their journey? He never talked to me very often, but when he did, he would send me a new tape of himself discussing his new plans."

"How?"

"Through that trapped door, of course. It only works one way. Until now."

I almost fell to my knees. "So, you're saying we can walk through that now, and we'll be free?"

"Don't get ahead of me." She snapped louder and feistier than before. While her boney yet youthful finger pointed to me, her puffy sleeve fell over her elbow to reveal burns and

156

bruises that her cruel father and potential partner must have left there on purpose for her to look at for the next two hundred years.

"Sorry," I mumbled.

"Now." She clasped her hands back together in front of her stomach as if nothing bothered her. "My nephew searched and searched until he found you three, but don't worry. He didn't jump to conclusions. He followed you for some time. Something about wasting human life began to bother him. I assumed that would happen at some point. Anyway, I didn't think any of you would buy going into a mysterious house alone. As far as I knew, these type of transactions don't usually occur in a home close to three hundred years old?"

Chess stood still and shrugged like somebody just asked her to tell them what gravity was made out of. "I - I."

"Sorry, silly me. Sliding off the subject. I don't have that many people to talk to. Excuse me. My nephew thought it would be best to fill Ren in on...mostly everything. He knew he was getting millions, and he knew that one of you would die. He informed us that he didn't have a preference on who. Just in case that makes you feel better." I didn't have to look over to see the steam rising from Chess's head. "Not only did he do that, but he actually hired a few people knowing you would con them. Just so he could get more information on you. We didn't want Ren to get too suspicious of what was *really* about to happen. Apparently the second you conned that poor man in the restaurant, he was so eager to tell us all about you, he insisted my nephew get a hold of...what's his name...John?"

Chess and I both nodded eager to hear more about John's involvement in the process. We prepared ourselves for the worst. "Did John know?"

"Oh please, you think I would risk having more people know? Absolutely not." I thought learning this would be the most relieving feeling. Nothing. Not a single burden lifted off my shoulders. Ren was the one keeping them down.

"Did Ren know anything about the tunnel?" Chess asked.

"Did it look like he knew anything about the tunnel?" Patience sneered. The answer was no, but any more visual vulnerability vibrating from us wasn't something we wanted to have held against us.

"You're lying," said Chess through an unscrewed jaw. "You have absolutely no proof. You're just trying to get a rise out of us."

"Am I?" Chess was right. She had no proof. But I could tell she was already preparing her evidence that was probably going to be at least somewhat convincing. "Who was the first person to suggest you take the job?" The answer was Ren, but neither of us said anything. "Who was the first person to suggest you go into the house?" Again, Ren. "Who was the most surprised when the house started to shake?" Probably Ren. "And who kept the quietest when deciphering my last clue?" Definitely Ren. I didn't want to tell Chess this, but we really needed to figure out how to get out of here instead of her trying to prove that Patience was lying.

"Would you just shut up?" I finally blurted out. "We just need to leave, lady."

"What about your money?" She was joking, right? But then again, the greedy side of me leaned in a little closer.

"Money? What money?"

Chess finally unfroze and said, "This *was* a goddamn job all along?"

"I have to reward you with something, don't I? You both did so splendidly!" This crazy bitch was being dead serious.

"Fine," I said. "Give us our money, and we'll leave. And when we leave, we won't tell anyone about you or this whole deal."

"Oh, my sweet." Jesus. That didn't sound good. Was this ever going to end? "You haven't finished the clue!"

"Yes, we have," Chess took a giant step closer to her like a vampire that could defy the laws of physics. "We've done everything you asked. We need to leave!"

"No!" If I didn't know any better, I would have said Patience grew four inches taller trying to tower over Chess. "You need to finish properly, and if you don't, you won't get your money, and you won't be able to leave. That's how it works. That's how it was always meant to be."

Her capitalist dictatorship almost made Chess and me break down in a full waterfall. It had been a while since I felt fear because of another human being. Chess didn't know what to say. Her chest stayed inflated not realizing it was time to exhale.

Patience stood in silence, probably working to intensify the circumstances, but her eyes sustained the same energy throughout the entire conversation.

"What do you want us to do?" Chess asked.

"Come with me." Patience widened her dimples with her closed-mouth smile. Once she turned around, dragging her beckoning index finger behind, she didn't need to check to see if we were following her. She simply walked right up to the trapped door, and opened it up without touching it.

"So, now you can open that?" Chess asked.

"Three came in, three can go out. You were right, by the way."

"Why you f-"

"Chess." Patience had more power than we thought, and that was definitely something Chess hadn't picked up on yet.

Patience disappeared through the trapped door before our eyes. I thought Chess would push me out of the way to escape, but instead she said, "You first," Chess whispered.

"Of course." I didn't argue. What more could she possibly do to us? And why was she so insistent on giving us money? Did she even have any? I was ready to jump through ten more mysterious trapped doors if it meant I could get out of here.

After crawling down the ladder and taking one last look at Ren's lifeless body, I felt my feet collide with the floor much sooner than I thought they would. The space surrounding me gave me the illusion there was no end to space anywhere on Earth. The walls weren't visible, they were so far away. I wondered how Patience knew where she was going. Was she ever able to come down here? But then again, her intuition must have been overpowering after two hundred years.

"OW!" I heard Chess holler. It almost sounded like she was going to break through the floor. But in usual Chess fashion, she shook it off like it was a bunch of rubbish and said, "Come on, let's go."

The walk to wherever we were going couldn't have been more than five minutes, but we strolled in complete silence. The fear should have sprouted from us throughout that walk, but Patience remained so calm, there wasn't any reason to...yet.

From what I could see along this path that might be considered a hall, the floor was made of stone, like the stone in the tunnel, and star-like lights hung from wherever they were hung from. It wasn't a ceiling per se, or maybe it was, but there wasn't much of a ceiling to look at. Only some sort of optical illusion that made the star lights look further away than they actually were, but the closer we got to it, I could finally see a small light right ahead of Patience similar to the one that led us through the tunnel. Not that it had the same shape or anything. Light is light, but I sensed the similarity.

"Right this way," Patience looked over her shoulder. A strange sound appeared out of nowhere after Patience turned back around. A sort of buzzing sound. I knew that sound. I'd heard that sound a million times over. Including in the tunnel, but could it really be?

"Is that-?" Chess muttered, squinting her eyes. Before we knew it, the dark surroundings and twinkling lights vanished and the tallest waterfall I'd ever seen materialized out of thin air.

"Holy-" But before I could finish, Chess already took the lead in the race to drink fresh water.

"Outta my way!" She almost pushed me over when I raced up next to her. I wasn't even in her way, and I wasn't sure why it was a race in the first place. This thing looked like it contained the entire Atlantic Ocean.

"I wouldn't do that if I were you," Patience calmly spoke. Chess turned around to show the anger seeping out of her eyes. She probably could have ripped out Patience's throat if she really wanted to.

"And why is that?" Chess asked.

"Actually, I'm really not quite sure. I just wouldn't risk it."

Like pulling teeth, I asked her, "Why wouldn't you risk it?"

"Take a look." Her hand gestured over the endless waterfall like she was thanking the audience for coming to her performance. "This is where everything from the tunnel and my chambers are flushed out. Every germ, every breath. This is the outhouse that dumps everything back into the atmosphere."

"Ew," Chess mumbled.

"But there's a chance that we'd be okay?" I asked.

"Of course," said Patience with a smile and a shrug. "But I don't know every detail of this environment. For instance,

I don't know why I can't eat, but you have to. I don't know why I've grown to emerge within the spirit of this tunnel. We've become one and the same. I have almost complete control over the tunnel, but I don't know how."

"We get it," I snapped, even though I was the one who had asked. "Why did you bring us down here? You want us to jump off that thing or something?"

Patience gave her smallest, tightlipped laugh yet. "Not exactly."

"Okay, enough," Chess blurted out of nowhere. "We're going to decide what happens now."

The laughter stopped. "You really think that, don't you?"

"I do. Because for the first time, during this entire bullshit, I don't believe you. Whatever it is that we need to do, I don't believe you. You were pretty convincing at first. I'll give you credit for that, but why can't we just jump out of here and escape. You already told us what this waterfall is for, and where it'll lead us. What are you gonna do to stop us?"

Where was Chess going with this? She could do a lot of shit to stop us. Had she not seen what this woman could do?

"Chess," I whispered.

"Stop." I don't know who she was speaking to, but she followed it with, "We're leaving. No deal. No money. We're done."

What? No money. To be fair, I didn't know how much money Patience was offering, but money was money, and the initial part of this adventure was supposed to be a job. Besides, what was John going to say if we came back with a bloody good story and no money?

"CHESS!" I screamed directly in her ear, so she wouldn't ignore me this time. "Are you bonkers? We need that money. Especially now that Ren's gone. How are we gonna keep operating without him?"

"Yeah," she surprisingly agreed. "We do. Now that we're a man down. We're gonna need more jobs, more money and more bullshit to deal with, but for now I wanna go home. This crazy bitch isn't trustworthy, and I don't wanna make a freaking deal with her after all of this."

My eyes had never locked so tightly with hers than in this moment, but it wasn't fear or anger in her soul. It was sadness. Pure depression.

"Chess, no." I didn't know how else to put it. We should be making this deal *because* Patience was untrustworthy. "Do I have to hold you down to make sure you don't do anything stupid? You might not think she can stop you, but I sure can, and you know that."

Now there was fear in her eyes.

"Have it your way," she whispered before she grabbed the bloody knife that was still in Patience's hand.

"Now we're talking," Patience laughed, or at least I think she did. I was rather distracted by the bright red knife pointed at my neck.

"You've got to be joking." Now there was fear bolted into *my* eyes, but I couldn't let Chess see it.

"You tell me," Chess responded. Instead of saying anything in return, I impulsively tried to whack the knife out of her hand, but Chess was always faster and stronger than she looked. The knife didn't drop, and in response, her foot kicked me straight in the stomach, which she knew was one of my sensitive spots. Damn it. My violent brawl with Chess had begun.

28:
CHESS

I won't lie. A part of me, a *big* part of me, enjoyed this. Currently, fighting was my outlet. Everything that I was angry about, and everyone that I held a grudge against was standing right in front of me, and I was beating the living shit out of them. The exhilarating energy almost made me laugh. This is what good television was made out of.

"Stop fighting me!" Paul deepened his voice as I swiped the knife right in front of his stomach.

"I will when you agree to leave with me!" I screamed through a tightened jaw.

"Not yet! Chess, we'll be okay!"

I didn't trust anyone. Not him, not Patience, and especially not myself. I've always been the queen of poor judgement. How was I gonna change now?

"You two have fun!" The crazy bitch hollered, twiddling her fingers. "I'll be right back." I didn't see if she vanished, but I assumed so from the sudden lack of heavy, creepy breathing.

"Chess, I promise you, we will figure this out. You just have to work with me!"

"I can't!" He dodged my uppercut into his left arm. "I don't trust you."

"When have you ever trusted me? When have you ever trusted anyone?" He wasn't helping his case and I didn't care. I wasn't trying to kill him. I didn't need any more blood on my hands, but I did need my control to be the dominant theme in this situation.

I ignored his question and continued to push him into a corner. Now *that's* a strong advantage when you're fighting a man almost twice your size. That is until he realizes what your plan is and strikes his foot into your stomach when you're distracted, looking past him.

"OOFF!" I almost did a graceful backwards somersault over my shoulder, but I snapped right back up with the knife still in my hand.

"Chess, this isn't gonna end well," said Paul.

"None of these potential scenarios have a happy ending. Ren is already dead. One of us is going to be next if we don't fight this bitch."

"THEN WHY ARE YOU FIGHTING ME?"

He had a point, but I wasn't done. My knife thought before I did and stabbed right into his bicep, but my stupid conscience pulled it right back out.

"AHHH," he screamed, but not for long. His hand stayed pressed against the bloody wound, but his energy never left him. "That was something." His anger almost grew to match mine. "Didn't see that coming."

"Clearly." My knife-held hand noticeably trembled with caution.

"What's your plan after you kill me?"

"I don't want to kill you."

"You didn't answer my question." Well, that's because I didn't have an answer. I had ideas, but not a thorough plan. Who knew what the hell was below that waterfall? I wouldn't be surprised if Patience was wrong about how to escape.

"Why do you care? You barely flinched when Ren keeled over." Before I almost broke my hip and kicked him in the face, I noticed his sudden confusion in his squinted eyes. Was he really that shocked that I actually cared about Ren being killed? Was that so hard to believe?

Paul adjusted his jaw only seconds before he charged at me with lightning speed that certainly wasn't there before. Otherwise, I would have been able to block the kick that whacked the knife right out of my hand. Great.

"What do you have to defend yourself now?" He boasted.

Idiot. I pulled out the small, dull pocket knife from my jacket that I used to almost kill the tiger. "I was thinking this." But before I could use it, Paul kicked again. I dodged this time, but I wasn't able to dodge the karate chop arm that followed.

"Damn it! I thought you didn't wanna fight." I kept my knees bent and my core flexed. Prepared for anything that he could throw at me.

"You're not leaving me much of a choice, are you?" And before I could answer, his shoulder shot straight into my stomach, causing me to fall over like the least valuable tackler in the NFL. I tried to knee him in his package, but I could only lay my feet flat on the floor and use my hips to push him off. *Then* I kicked him in his package. "JESUS!" He would have fallen over if he wasn't already on the dirty floor. "WHAT WAS THAT FOR?"

"Just because I know you can hold me down, doesn't mean you're gonna win this fight." I stood up straight before I realized I had the advantage now. The waterfall was maybe a hundred feet away from me. According to Patience, it was the only exit out of the tunnel that she knew of. What could be so dangerous if I left through there? Paul was down, and my adrenaline was pumping. It was time to run.

"CHESS! NO!" Paul screamed, but I ignored him. He didn't care what happened to me. Why should I care about what happened to him? I had a plan of escape, and it was almost fully executed.

"Have fun getting fucked over again!" I laughed the second before I shamelessly and fearlessly took the biggest dive, head first, into what looked like an endless waterfall.

The wind tingled against my skin. My tangled hair blew past my neck. I started falling faster and faster until some sort of energy swooped me up in a circle. This was it. I was leaving this godforsaken hell hole. Or that's what I thought until this energetic force shot me back into the air and onto the rocky platform right next to the waterfall.

"AH!" I noticed that my shoulder dislocated after the third or fourth roll along the ground. Finally, I came to a halt, which only gave me a chance to scream more. "AHHHH!"

"Oh," I heard a familiar voice say. "So *that's* what it does." Patience stood there, almost disappointed she missed all the fun.

Paul's footsteps echoed in my ear before I felt his hands grabbing a hold of me and helping me up.

"Is your shoulder dislocated?" he asked.

"No shit, dude," I responded.

"Good!" Without any warning he squeezed my shoulders together with his massive arms and slammed my shoulder back in its socket.

"GOD FUCKING….AHHH!"

"That was a bloody satisfying sound." I really hoped he wasn't referring to the popping sound my shoulder made that made me squirm more than the actual pain, but of course, he was.

"Are you done?" Patience asked.

There was no other choice. I had to do what she said. *We* had to do what she said. I should've known by now that's how this tunnel worked.

"Fine," I said to her, barely opening my lips.

"Splendid," she hopped, clapping her hands together. "Excuse me for my absence. I was preparing the final challenge." Man, I didn't like the sound of that. "Just for fun, and because I can now, I think I'll give you a little bit more than just a single word for a clue." I *really* didn't like the sound of that. Especially with the menacing look on her face. She was way too excited about this. "Let's just say, I'm gonna need some help moving out."

I was not about to bring a moving truck into this place for this asshole. The sudden shake in the floor didn't necessarily tell me what I needed to know, but it absolutely debunked my first theory.

"What the -" Paul mumbled. This was - what? The third earthquake of the trip? But nonetheless, it became the least of our concerns when, in the distance, a mob of angry tigers came slowly prancing toward us. And yes, you heard me right. Not a singular tiger. *Tigers.* Even better, they looked damn hungry.

"Do you hear that?" Paul asked.

"No, I'm currently distracted, believe it or not." The both of us almost tripped trying to carefully walk backwards.

"Okay, it's just that I think I hear those bees coming from up above us." He was right, the dimly lit ceiling was covered with those goddamn, giant bees. And we still had no idea what the hell to do.

"Any ideas?" I asked Paul.

"I guess just run." I didn't argue. Somehow, we both started running in the opposite directions, but we didn't have a destination. Wherever we were, the room was bigger than any football stadium I'd ever seen. I guess running in circles was our only option.

From the corner of my sweaty eye, I could see Patience standing exactly how and where she was before, completely unaffected. The magic held within Patience protected her from harm.

Crack! We heard from above, because of course we did. I didn't have to look up to know that the ceiling was about to start crumbling down. All of the scarring memories from this haunting journey were about to come out for their encore. And if that wasn't enough, the pool below the waterfall did something I wasn't expecting from a bottomless pit. It was starting to *overflow*. Suddenly it hit me. The answer. Everything that tortured us, everything that tried to kill us, had to leave with us, and we had to let it happen.

"PAUL!" I screamed. "PAUL! WE HAVE TO LET THEM ATTACK US!"

"ARE YOU MAD?" This was gonna take some convincing.

"THAT'S THE ONLY WAY! THAT'S WHAT THE CLUE MEANS!" I grabbed him by the arm. I could tell the thought sunk into him too. He knew I was right.

"OKAY, FINE!" The tigers looked even more hungry up close, and the bees were much louder than I remembered. I'd never been so scared in my entire life, let alone the entire journey. Paul took my hand as we closed our eyes and let the closest tiger to us claw us to the ground.

"AHHH!" Paul screamed louder than me, but we were both already in too much physical and mental pain to feel any more pain. A few bees managed to squirm their way to sting me in the neck and stomach, and probably way more places, but I couldn't tell.

The moment finally came where the one tiger that wanted me all to itself was about to go for her first bite right to my face. I could see it in her eyes, but before they could, the water sucked us all into what felt like a giant vacuum cleaner. I looked over to see if Paul survived the attack, and when I saw his eyes and mouth wide open, and watched him trying to scream into the water, I sure as hell got my answer.

The icy water made me immediately start shivering, and the speed we were being pulled at certainly didn't help. On top of that, I didn't take a deep enough breath before we unexpectedly went under. The tigers, fallen parts of the stone ceiling, and bees all faded away into the distance as Paul and I continued to be pulled backwards through the water. My eyes couldn't stay open. Mainly from the lack of oxygen, but the water grew darker and darker. Wherever we were going, it would have to wait until I woke back up...hopefully.

29:
PAUL

Chess's whimpers forced me to open my eyes. Once again, the brightness of the sun pierced into my soul, continuing to drain every bit of sleep I had had over the past few days.

"Chess?" I croaked. "Chess, are you okay? Can you hear me?"

The attempt at keeping her conscious thankfully worked, but only resulted in a scratchy, "Yeah," as a response. "Where are you? I can't see."

I didn't want to admit that I couldn't see either, but the more I wobbled my bleeding head back and forth, the more awake I felt. It wasn't until I shook my sleeping feet that I realized there was a chunk of my thigh missing above the knee on my left side. Nothing deadly, but I didn't need to see it to know.

"Ahhhh!" I screeched. The uncontrollable urges to scream came from my anxiety about what this could medically result in, not the pain.

"Paul! What's wrong?" She still couldn't see me, and I couldn't speak for her, but I could barely focus my hearing on the noises around me. No. It took a bloody truck to honk its horn at us in order for us to realize we were lying in the middle of a road.

"Oh, shit, SHIT!" I cursed trying to pull myself up and get Chess out of the way too. The truck was kind enough to drive around us. What a gentleman, but it didn't come without a lovely flipping of the bird. American, therefore rude, of course.

"Paul? Paul?" She kept mumbling.

"I'm right here. Ahhh! - uh - I've got you." The best I was able to do was to get on my aching knees and pull her out of the road. Luckily, she gained enough consciousness in order to use her feet and push along with my assistance.

"I'm fine. I'm fine." She couldn't stop repeating her words over and over again.

"Chess, neither of us is fine."

"I know. Now, would you shut up?" Her dynamism came from nowhere.

"Yes, yeah - but we need to get to hospital. Now." I meant what I said, but I didn't believe for an instant it was going to happen. From where we were sprawled out on the side of the road, I didn't recognize anything, and as a result, I was drawn to do something rather irrational. "Chess, what's my ex-wife's name?"

"What?"

"What's my ex-wife's name?"

"Jane!" No. That wasn't enough. Like Chess said before, Patience had access to endless knowledge. There was nothing I could ask her to be one-hundred percent sure it was her. "Paul, I know what you're trying to do. Once again, you're just gonna have to trust me. How many times do I have to tell you this?"

"Why?" My shoulders and feet popped with my voice. "We don't have to stick together anymore. Are we even in business anymore?"

"Ya know." I always hated it when she started her sentences with those words. "I don't think what we do qualifies as 'business'. At least not anymore."

"Oh God, whatever could have changed?"

We didn't say anything to each other for the next few minutes. It felt like hours though. During my silence, I went over the next chapter in my life, detail by detail. What if we were to adjust the business instead of dropping it all together? Smaller cons. Only easy stuff. John was clean now. He could take over Ren's job.

"Don't even think about it," Chess finally broke the silence.

"What?"

"We can't do this anymore. Look at the trouble it got us into. We need to be more discreet in our lives. What if she comes after us again?"

"Why would she do that?"

"I don't know!" Nothing in her voice sounded familiar. She adopted a different type of anger in her voice. "We still don't understand anything about this. We could be in jeopardy for the rest of our lives for all we know."

I didn't leave a beat before I said, "No." Just like that. "No. We can't let that happen. We're smart. We're skilled.

Maybe Patience was right about Ren, and maybe we should stop our scams, but we still need to stay connected."

"What do you mean?"

"After we figure out where we are, go to hospital, we can go our separate ways. But just in case we need each other, we can figure out a way to discreetly alert each other. Okay?"

Disappointment arose within her. She didn't want to admit it, but Chess's new life was coming to an end whether she liked it or not.

"Fine," she responded. "Let's just get to a hospital."

We had to go to four different stores in order for someone to tell us where the closest hospital was. I suppose a bleeding, limping man wasn't persuasive enough for some people. After a few hours, we finally reached the nearest hospital and fortunately sat in the waiting room for less than two minutes.

"Harriet?" The nurse announced.

"God, I am so not in the mood," Chess whispered. "Over here!"

Eventually we ended up two doors down from one another in the same hospital wing. My knee needed some drugs and only a few stitches. My back, however, was a different story, and to top it all off, explaining what happened to us wasn't my most fine-tuned performance.

"We just woke up on the side of the road. Somebody probably kidnapped us," I told the doctor.

"And then spat you back out?" She didn't seem convinced.

"I suppose so."

"Do you want to file a police report?" Absolutely no concern vibrated in her voice. It was more of a robotic, standard, repetitive, procedural tone.

"No!" I spoke way too quickly. "We're okay. We just wanna forget about all of this."

Still, not one word that came out of my mouth sounded convincing to this woman. But there was something else. Something discomforting. She looked at me like I had done her dirty. As if we had a long history of backstabbing each other. Doing what I do for a living, many people looked at me like that. Lord, I hoped she hadn't been one of our clients or victims. We often ripped off both clients and victims if I'm being honest.

The next few hours were the most peaceful hours I had had in a long time. Not just because of the lack of murderous rocks, tigers, and bees surrounding me, but because I enjoyed the annoying white noise fluttering about. The loud ringing at the nurse's station down the hall, the footsteps evenly squeaking one by one. Not that I was the biggest fan of hospitals, but it was the closest thing that I had to normal in what felt like way too long. That and I felt so bloody clean. Between the I.V. and clean hospital gown, I could have been twenty years old again for all I knew.

Just when I felt an urge of fatigue coming on, I heard three light knocks on my door followed by three loud ones. A quality only Chess possessed.

"Yo," she said.

"Don't ever say 'yo' again," I responded.

"Make me." Not that funny of a laugh, but I cracked a smile anyway. "I just -" She looked around to make sure no one was listening. "Have people been asking you questions?"

"You have no idea."

"I beg to differ." Without permission, she walked up to my bed and sat on it. "I told them we were attacked on the street we were found on."

"Well, shit." I was trapped. Back in the cave again. "I told them we were kidnapped somewhere, and then we woke up on that road."

"Whatever." Classic response from her, but even worse now. If there was any absence of fear, she thought she was invincible, so it would never bother her as it would a normal person.

"What's that supposed to mean?"

"They're doctors, not cops. Please, the amount of times I went to the hospital for alcohol poisoning in college, no one even asked if I had someone to drive me home afterward. They don't care. I just don't want them to go around talking. Just give them an answer and just shut them up."

"It's a little late for that, don't you think?" Not up for more pointless banter, I rolled over onto my side. Apparently, that didn't drop any hints to Chess.

"You get what I mean," she said.

172

"Listen." I already didn't fancy the sound of that. "I think we should abide by what we said after we woke up." Her motionless face stood as it was; exhausted and discontent.

"I know. I didn't think any different. Why would I?"

"I don't know." We sat in silence for a little while. Not awkward silence, just depressing, filled with reflection.

"What are you gonna do now?" I was hoping she wasn't gonna ask me this. I had a few ideas. None of which I wanted to share with her.

"I don't know. Perhaps go back to England." Well, that was a slip of the tongue. The funny thing was, I sort of meant it.

"With the money from Patience?"

"Chess, you don't seriously think she's actually going to give that to us, do you?"

Chess crossed her arms and leaned up against the wall before she said, "Really? After all that, you don't want the money?"

"Oh, I want the money. I just know she's not going to give it to us. She would have found us by now, and I don't want to ever be in her presence again. Her nephew, or whoever enchanted that place, probably just wanted extra security before she got out. That's why she made us do that last level. She was never going to give us any money."

"Good point...So you're really going back to England?"

"Chess, no offense, but my England is not your Santa Barbara. If I return to East London, I'll have to go to therapy for a while, but I can get through it. If you return to Santa Barbara, you'll be arrested."

"Or get the living shit beaten out of me."

"Ah, yes. That too." Neither of us laughed, but I wanted to. Just a little. Maybe if I did, it would make going back to England easier. I could make a life there for myself. If I tried.

"Sorry I bothered you. I'll go back to my room. I probably shouldn't be walking anyway." Before she passed the door frame, she barely leaned over her shoulder and said, "Take care, Paul," without an ounce of remorse, because of course. But before she could exit the door, the doctor purposely got in her way. Bugger. Big mistake.

"Miss Rig-" she said before Chess interrupted her.

"Excuse me!"

"Miss Rigby, there are a few things we need to discuss with you and your partner."

"Partner? Please tell me you're implying the word business in there, 'cause I am really not in the freaking mood."

The doctor tilted her head implying she really wasn't in the mood either. "Yes, I am actually."

The worst thing about being in hospital with a heart monitor on was the fact that the doctors knew when something was wrong, or when you were lying, or even worse; both.

"What do you need to discuss?" I softly asked her, trying desperately to cover up my heart palpitations.

"I was hoping you could tell me if this was you or not." And with a single turn of an iPad, our lives were not ours. A picture from an online newspaper showed Chess and me at the restaurant with Mr. Beau. More specifically, it shows us conning him. We should have known. Shit, we really should have known. Of course, we were set up.

"Yes, that's us," said Chess with confidence. "Why do you want to know?" Oh, so that's how we were gonna play this? The dumb card.

"Miss, did you read the headline?"

It read; *CONS SCAM BEAU IN HIS OWN RESTAURANT!*

Shit.

"That's a goddamn lie." Chess continued to play along. "Mr. Beau has no proof. Where is his claim coming from?"

The crooked smile the doctor planted on her face told me she had a solid answer for that question. "He said he knew something was wrong when he went to look at the address you gave on the website and nothing but a CVS was there. But apparently the website led the F.B.I. to a computer that's registered to a man named Ren Patel. Any chance you know him?"

"No," Chess snapped without missing a beat.

"Really?" The crooked smile never left her face. "Because they also have a picture of all three of you entering his car outside the restaurant that same night." She flipped the page to reveal just that. There was no getting out of this, but Chess only continued to make it worse.

"So, he *did* set us up! He's lying to you!"

"The police will deal with that later, Miss Rigby. But before they get here, would you like to tell me where Mr. Patel is?"

No. She wouldn't. She had no reason to but it's possible. If Patience still had Ren's body, she could very well frame us, and she would do a damn good job too.

"How are we supposed to know where he is?" Chess naturally answered. "The last time we saw him was right before we got kidnapped and concussed. He's probably at home, so tell the police to check there."

"Oh, the police did. They just called, he's not there. I hope the news will keep us all updated. I'll be eager to know how you both handle prison." The doctor wanted this. The likelihood of her going home to her significant other and jumping around screaming about how superior she was for finding and reporting us was pathetically high.

"Again, you have no proof."

"We'll leave that up to the police." And just like a cheesy scene in a soap opera, two overly tall, bulky police officers walked through the door.

Bloody hell.

After I was discharged from the hospital two hours later, the police were nice enough to let me put my pants and trousers back on so at least my ass wasn't hanging out from my hospital gown.

I could tell this wasn't Chess's first time getting arrested, but something about her aesthetic gave me the impression it had been a while. Probably before her incident in Santa Barbara. She knew her life was over now. There was no escaping and moving halfway across the country. We were stuck. I was stuck with her. If we were cleared, I would probably be fine. Would Chess? Probably not, and for some godforsaken reason, I felt as if I owed her something.

"How much longer until we get to the police station?" Chess asked after sitting handcuffed in the back of the police car for roughly two minutes.

"Don't worry about it," the bald officer responded. Another minute went by, and Chess made a sort of whimper that was probably her specialty as a teenager.

"Chess," I whispered, trying to get her attention while trying to get her to shut up too. "I know we said all that stuff about going our separate ways and such, but I'll do what I can to make sure you don't stay in there for long."

"For long?"

"Chess, that's probably the best that I'll be able to do. So, take it or leave it."

"And how are you gonna do that?"

"I know...people." She made that noise again, but added a little huff to it. Although, her eyes told me she was hiding something. Even better, I think she wanted to tell me. "What?"

"Just wait. We're coming to a stop light." Bloody hell. She knew these doors were locked, right?

"Chess, do you -" But before I could finish, she stabbed me with something. Or more...poked? "Ow." She gave me a look that told me to shut up before the cops could hear. Then, I looked down to see something rough, red, and somewhat large engulfed in Chess's cuffed hand.

A copper rock.

"How? - What? - Do you think it could bust through these doors?" We approached the stop light while Chess pulled her cuffed hands under her bum and past her legs.

"Wanna find out?"

EPILOGUE:
PATIENCE

The silence still trapped the loneliness barred within me. Freedom rang just as boring as prison, but still. I had choices. Choices I didn't have before. The only exciting endeavor I had the pleasure of experiencing was food. The taste of food, the benefits of food, even the consequences of eating too much food. There would never be enough of it. I learned to stop craving food decades ago when time was standing still for me, but it only took looking at an apple to turn me into a hungry lion.

Looking outside my window was stranger than being trapped inside a cave for two hundred years. Everything was different. The houses, the color schemes, even the dogs looked bigger. Or maybe most dogs were simply fat and plump these days. My, how American food had changed.

After staring out the window and eating eight bars of chocolate, I finally accepted nature's invitation to take a long walk. It was calling me for a while, but I didn't appreciate its impatient attitude.

Not many people filled the streets, but every single person knitted their eyebrows while staring blankly at me. I knew why. Most modern-day humans weren't accustomed to seeing a nineteen-year-old girl with messy ringlets and a long, pink, velvet dress. However, it wouldn't be the slightest bit appropriate for me to adapt to their nonsense fashion statements. Why should I? I was not one of them. Nor would I ever be.

I let the discomfort bother me for a little while. Who knew how much longer I was going to last? What if my cave cursed me and I could turn to stone at any moment? No. My father would do something much more dramatic than that. Maybe crumple me into dust, scarred into a pile on the kitchen floor for the next owners to scrape off. I would have asked Samuel if he had any suggestions if he hadn't disappeared before I came knocking on the door. He always did come off as cowardly to me. Maybe he thought it would be *him* that took my place. Now I was thinking that wouldn't be such a bad idea.

I could have walked for twice as long as I did, but I wanted another chocolate bar. Seems it was my nephew's favorite. He had two more packages of them after all.

The walk home turned into a pensive therapy session. What was I to do now? Did women work these days? How did they go about that? Did I even need a job? Or did my nephew leave enough money for me? However, that wasn't the most prominent dilemma that stood out to me. What if my cave craved my return? My aunt's alchemy did give it the power to think for itself. That was the only reason I stayed there after her death. Maybe if I stayed away. But where would I go? I had no more family left. If anything, my cave would suck *somebody* back into its possession. That's what it was designed for after all.

The next two chocolate bars were my favorite. Now, I was familiar with the taste. Excitement and anticipation filled every ounce of me, seeing a fully wrapped chocolate bar as silly as it was. And right as I finished the last bite of my second bar, a strange ringing noise ruptured through the entire house.

Ding-dong!

Then it rang again. And again, until my shaking eyes saw two people standing at the front door. They must have found a way to make that atrocious noise flutter about my business, but of course, I didn't want to be rude. They were an elderly couple. They deserved my respect.

With instinctive caution, I opened the door, still skeptical of what they could have possibly wanted.

"Hello!" The old woman cheerfully held up what looked like a delicious cherry pie. "We're from next door, we just moved in."

The old man next to her smiled and said, "I'm Clark Hudson, and this is my wife, Betty. We live in that house right there. Just moved in." He lifted his wrinkled, elderly finger to the house right next to mine.

"Really?" I didn't mean to come off so coarse, but they were rather overly friendly for my taste.

"We thought we would come over with some gifts," said Betty, anxiously handing her pie to me.

"Oh, my." I almost dropped it, I was so caught off guard.

"We don't know anyone around here," said Clark. "So, we thought we would introduce ourselves to the whole neighborhood."

My smile cracked without any real intention, but it was their fault. They walked up to the wrong house.

"Is that so?"

ACKNOWLEDGMENTS:

You! Yes you! I want to start off by saying thank you for traveling through the tunnel with me, Chess, Ren, and Paul. Although, I'm sure I was much better company than those three.

Thank you to my dad, Doug for putting up with me and editing this book. Thank you to my sister, Taryn who still hasn't read my first book. Thank you to the rest of my family, because I'm pretty sure they all finished reading my first book.

Thank you to Olivia, for designing the amazing cover. Thank you to anyone who has ever given me feedback on my writing or corrected my grammar. And thank you to Patience for hopefully not giving anyone nightmares.

Made in the USA
Monee, IL
24 December 2021